Born in Montreal, Emmanuel Kattan currently heads the British Council's 'Our Shared Future' initiative in New York. He was previously Head of Communications at the UN Alliance of Civilizations and the Commonwealth Secretary-General's speechwriter in London, UK. He also worked at the Quebec Delegation in London, where he managed academic relations and student exchange programs. Emmanuel studied in Oxford as a Rhodes Scholar and is a graduate of the University of Montreal and the Ecole des Hautes Etudes en Sciences Sociales in Paris. He lives in New York with his wife and two sons. *Love Alone* is his first novel.

Books of Merit

Love Alone

Love

Emmanuel Kattan

Translated by Sheila Fischman

THOMAS ALLEN PUBLISHERS
TORONTO

© Les Éditions du Boréal 2008
Translation © 2011 by Sheila Fischman

All rights reserved. No part of this work may be reproduced or transmitted in any form or by any means—graphic, electronic, or mechanical, including photocopying, recording, taping, or information storage and retrieval systems—without the prior written permission of the publisher, or in the case of photocopying or other reprographic copying, a licence from the Canadian Copyright Licensing Agency.

Catalogage avant publication de Bibliothèque et Archives Canada

Kattan, Emmanuel, 1968–
[Nous seuls. English]
    Love alone / Emmanuel Kattan ; translated by Sheila Fischman.

Translation of: Nous seuls.
ISBN 978-0-88762-810-8

I. Fischman, Sheila II. Titre. III. Titre: Nous seuls. English.

PS8621.A68N6813   2011   C843'.6   C2011-903257-0

Cover design: Michel Vrána
Cover photo (water pistol): Spaulin / istockphoto.com
Text design: Gordon Robertson

Published by Thomas Allen Publishers,
a division of Thomas Allen & Son Limited,
390 Steelcase Road East,
Markham, Ontario L3R 1G2 Canada

www.thomasallen.ca

 Canada Council for the Arts

The publisher gratefully acknowledges the support of The Ontario Arts Council for its publishing program.

We acknowledge the support of the Canada Council for the Arts, which last year invested $20.1 million in writing and publishing throughout Canada.

We acknowledge the Government of Ontario through the Ontario Media Development Corporation's Ontario Book Initiative.

We acknowledge the financial support of the Government of Canada through the Canada Book Fund for our publishing activities.

We acknowledge the financial support of the Government of Canada, through the National Translation Program for Book Publishing, for our translation activities.

11 12 13 14 15   5 4 3 2 1

Text printed on a 100% PCW recycled stock

Printed and bound in Canada

Our path is a meandering thread that we follow, disoriented, unknowingly crisscrossing back to where we were, unsure whether we are forging ahead or heading back—and when we die, God pulls the thread and suddenly our whole life becomes one straight line.

—VANUDRINE SINHA

Love Alone

1

Battersea, London, 6 November 2001

A man and a woman are walking along the Thames with a child. In his right hand the boy, who could be three or four proudly holds his father's car key and now and then hops up and down to see the boats go by on the other side of the parapet. To tease his parents, he sometimes stops and pretends to fling the key into the river. After the fourth time, the mother tries to take it from him, but too late: the child has thrown it over the wall. At once, the parents bend forward and spot the key some four metres down, wedged between two rocks. The father advances silently until he comes to a ladder that leads to the embankment. As he walks along the pebbles covered in silt, he observes objects washed up by the tide: an emaciated fish being devoured by black flies; a plastic bottle full of water weeds; a shoe; an old rug; a battery; a muddy pacifier. Close to the rocks he carefully picks up the key with his handkerchief. On his way back to the ladder, he spots the shoe again. It is pointing upwards, the heel sunk in the mud. Intrigued, he comes closer, to push it out of the way with his toe. He feels some resistance and that's when he notices, standing out under the blue-green surface of the water, the pallor of a body. He thinks he can make out the shape of a woman: rounded thighs, sagging breasts and, framing a face masked with seaweed, long blond hair. He stands there motionless for a few moments, eyes focused on the shoe. It is the child's voice that brings him back to the world. Standing on the stone wall, radiant, the boy shows his father his new balloon. The father starts running to the ladder, slipping on the shingle beach, his feet sinking into the mud. At the top of the ladder, gasping for breath, he murmurs to his wife, "It's horrible, there's a body!" She stares at him, taken aback. "Honestly, there's a dead woman on the shore." She hesitates another few moments; she has never seen him so pale. She gestures to him to stay with the child and walks away, digging in her purse for her cellphone. A few minutes later she comes back and whispers in his ear, "It's all right, the police are coming." The child tugs at his mother's sleeve.

"What's wrong with Daddy?"

"He's just a little tired, sweetheart, don't worry."

"Daddy sick! Daddy medicine!" the child exclaims.

She looks at the boy, smiling faintly.

"Yes, darling, your Daddy isn't feeling well. We'll go home now."

*

New York, 18 September 2000

In the end, I'll be rather sad to leave New York. Finally I've become attached to this city. When I first came here nine years ago, New York was merely a refuge, a cold and unattractive place. I felt lost and I was relieved not to find anything here that could help me to find myself. In New York more than anywhere else, one exists for no one unless one exists first, inordinately, for oneself. And I had stopped wanting that. I'd become a kind of robot, wandering aimlessly through the teeming streets, desiring nothing. I'd spend the afternoon in a Starbucks watching the people come and go, and the night slumped in front of the TV, steeped in words and laughter I could hardly recognize. When I looked inside myself I saw only the past, the sheer size of what I had lost. The future was the future with him. Without him, only memories were left.

Gradually, though, I got used to my new life. I started working in Dad's gallery, in SoHo. I planned receptions, hung around with the artists we helped launch. I went out a lot. New York no longer seemed so hostile. I still felt like an outsider but I was fascinated, virtually seduced by the gigantic avenues, the concrete canyons, the vast perspectives where humans feel crushed, minuscule, insignificant. New Yorkers themselves didn't seem so unpleasant. Instead of judging them, I tried to recognize myself in them. I too was a little unconventional, a little lost, self-absorbed and always ready to invent a new life for myself. I scrutinized my father's circle—all the artists who sailed from dream to dream as if their past, weighing more and more, was no obstacle, as if they were still making their first attempts—and I thought to myself that basically I was not very different from them.

What I'll miss most is not the city but the memories I leave here. They are in all the places that have gradually become my everyday landscape: the Chelsea boutiques, the labyrinthine bookstores near Washington Square, the fruit-seller from whom I buy a banana every morning on my way to the gallery. I'll remember Dylan's Candy Bar where, nostalgic for the candies of my childhood, I went now and then to stock up on jujubes; and the Italian café on York Avenue whose sign claimed that they sold "the best ice cream this side of Milan." I'll remember reading on the edge of the willow-lined pond in Central Park, and my evening strolls along the East River. I will also remember the disturbing majesty of the Brooklyn Bridge, which I never crossed without thinking how easy it would be to step over the parapet and jump.

New York, 20 *September* 2000

Half-past two a.m. I can't get to sleep. Maybe it's the excitement about leaving. I'm probably more worried than I'm willing to admit to myself.

I tried to fall asleep in front of the TV. Didn't work. I watched a horror film from the sixties. Back then it probably would have been normal to think it was bad. But time bestows a certain charm on films like that. They turn into riddles to be decoded. Intelligence and the spirit of invention, invisible when they merge into the spirit of the time, suddenly surface like luminous insights, and the worst clichés get back their flavour, because they've long ago stopped pervading our world. The plot was unbelievable. Pylons struck by some mysterious power had come to life and started to stalk the city, some American megalopolis or other, destroying everything in their path. From their great metal arms dangled bits of electrical wire that whipped the inhabitants as they went by. There were sounds of twisting metal, sparks, fire and, most of all, screaming.

Panic-stricken women were running in every direction while brave, phlegmatic men with clenched jaws saved children imprisoned by buildings in flames.

    I was grateful because the film made me laugh. Quietly, for a long time, with pleasure. It was the first time since my father's death.

*

It was one of the memories Séverine came back to most often. One summer evening she and Antoine were strolling through the streets of Cannes. At the end of rue d'Antibes, they had turned onto avenue du Maréchal Juin and ended up in a small park surrounded by plane trees where young neighbourhood mothers brought their children to play in the afternoon when it was too hot for the beach. Sitting on swings they talked without looking at one another, eyes lost in the shadowy light. Nothing exceptional happened that night, but to Séverine it seemed, though she couldn't have said why, that something could have happened—and that her life might perhaps have been transformed.

    They had met the year before, during the summer of 1989. Sent by their parents to Cork to learn English, they had been the only two French people in a diverse community of German, Spanish, Italian and Japanese teens. During the first days, small groups had formed

Love Alone / 7

and whether it was through their desire to stand out or simply by oversight, they'd been excluded. Neither was very enthusiastic at the thought of spending the summer holidays in a classroom, but they'd been able to accept the discipline of homework, reviews and practical exercises more willingly than the others. Antoine's parents had given up their own holidays to pay for his classes and he didn't want to disappoint them. As for Séverine, she was thinking about her career, and learning English seemed to her essential.

They had gotten into the habit of having lunch together and in the evening after classes, they went walking in the old city or along the River Lee. To ease their consciences, they tried to communicate in English. As they spoke it equally badly, neither one minded making up words and manhandling grammar, punctuating their conversation with French words when they couldn't make themselves understood. They felt as if they were performing a poorly translated play, full of misinterpretations, funny and ridiculous in spite of itself.

These artificial exchanges had brought them together. The effort needed to use a language that was not theirs had lifted the barrier of rules and agreements that are generally compulsory in one's mother tongue. For them, words were pure tools, drained of any emotion, any past. When they described their feelings in English, it seemed to them that they were talking about someone else. Then they could speak freely about their private lives, about conflicts with their parents and their amorous setbacks, and not worry about sounding ridiculous. Antoine, who at seventeen had spent most of his teenage years dreaming about love but had never gone beyond a kiss, opened his heart about the precarious nature of desire and the unreliability of emotions. He had a lot to say about the secret love that he'd developed for a girl in his class in secondary school, about the hope stirred in him by something she'd said during their drawing class and the highs and lows his emotions had undergone since. She was not particularly pretty, he knew that, but he liked the simplicity of her gaze, her long graceful hands, her nonchalant posture. Most appealing were the half-smiles she sometimes gave him in response to his questions: cedillas would appear, one at each corner of her lips, giving her an exasperated look and, he thought, a certain nobility that both intimidated and excited him. Her name was Laetitia Bohémier and Antoine pronounced her name with obvious pleasure, as if it were a way of getting close to her, of entering her life.

When he wasn't talking about Laetitia, Antoine was questioning himself—about his future, about the unwillingness of his parents and his friends to understand. Séverine listened with curiosity. Unlike Antoine, she no longer expended so much energy wondering how others saw her. Early on, Séverine had given up the cumbersome uncertainties that sometimes gave adolescence its aura of arrogant wisdom and gloomy pride. She had rid her dreams of whatever they contained that was disproportionate, excessive, implausible, leaving only reasonable aspirations, the image of a comfortable and peaceful life that nothing would stir. Understanding that if love is to be great it must also be complicated, she had put together for herself the reassuring vision of a perfectly ordinary relationship, as harmonious and calm as a desert of ice. For her, love had the peaceful appearance of silent habits, of the rather dull moments of everyday life, reproduced to infinity. She took pleasure in imagining the small rituals that would order her life: the quick morning kisses exchanged before leaving for work, dinners shared in front of the television, Friday night movies, Sunday mornings reading the papers in bed. In fact, she was dreaming not about a man but about a couple whose clear, smooth life would perpetuate itself, confident and indifferent to the world.

*

New York, 24 September 2000

At first, when people asked me why I'd come to New York, I said that it was to join my father. "He invited me to come and work in the gallery with him." That explanation seemed to satisfy everyone and soon people stopped questioning me. To tell the truth though it was mainly because I wanted to get out of Paris. I had to forget that break, had to put some distance between him and me and everything that kept his memory alive in me.

I wanted to start over, to "turn the page," as we say. But to build a new life you need plans. I lived all those years in New York with my back turned to the future. I'd come here to forget, but I was constantly allowing my memories to rush back into me. All my thoughts, even the most trivial, ended up taking me back to him. He was more present in that city where he'd never set foot than in Montmartre, where I could have run into him at any corner. The past was greater and more cumbersome than all my dreams.

New York, 27 September 2000

I often thought about Dad's death. I imagined myself wakened by the telephone in the middle of the night.

I heard a slow, solemn voice, slightly weary perhaps, ask, "May I speak to Ms. Judith Thomas?" Automatically, but already terrified, I answered, "Speaking." And before I heard the devastating words, I anticipated them—perhaps so that I wouldn't hear them, or with the absurd hope of warding them off: "Ms. Thomas, I have some bad news." I saw myself standing, gripping the receiver, unable to speak. Words seemed suddenly beyond my reach. And the voice at the other end moved away too. All I heard was a murmur: "Ms. Thomas? Ms. Thomas! Can you hear me? Are you all right?"

I rarely repeated the same scenario. Sometimes he died after a long illness, sometimes in his sleep. And at other times he was travelling and I had to bring his body home. There were also a thousand practical details that I had to take care of. I mentally wrote the announcements, closed the bank accounts, chose a tombstone. Then came the condolences. Faces unknown to me filed past, whispering, as if they knew that I wasn't listening. With their arched eyebrows, their sorrowful smiles, they seemed to want to express their helplessness—their inability to express or to feel anything at all.

I felt guilty about drawing up these fictions, as if they were incestuous dreams. But I couldn't help it. I tried to resist, to focus my attention on something else, but as soon as I had *touched* that thought, so to speak, it swept me up irresistibly in its whirlwind. When Dad kissed me in the morning after one of those tormented nights when I'd seen him dead a thousand times, I dared not meet his gaze. I was even a little angry with him. I thought to myself that he should have been able to see inside me. His silence reminded me that I had no right to his benevolence.

Needless to say, things didn't happen as they did in my dreams. No middle-of-the-night phone call, no lengthy illness, no body to bring home. I discovered him myself more than a month ago, collapsed on the kitchen floor. I'd waited for him at the gallery all morning and as he wasn't answering the phone I'd decided to go to his place at lunch. In the elevator I took out a comb to fix my hair, and it was when I looked in the mirror that I realized how worried I was. I had to ask the concierge to let me in.

I stood on the doorstep for a few seconds and called to him several times, as if I were afraid of catching him at a private moment. I went first to his bedroom. The bed was unmade, but there was nothing alarming about that. The curtains were still drawn though, and the clothes he'd worn the day before were still on the back of his easy chair. The concierge had followed me into the bathroom, then the living room.

Total silence. Outside the kitchen I kept my hands on the doorknob for a long moment. I tried in vain to remember what we'd said on the phone the night before. Had he wished me goodnight? Had he mentioned his plans for today? Suddenly those details seemed very important. I felt a wave of heat come up from my chest; I could hear nothing but the sound of my breathing.

When I opened the door I saw him stretched out on the floor, behind the counter. His right cheek was pressed against the tile; there was a dribble of saliva from his partly open mouth. I didn't cry out. I had feared this moment so much that I no longer had the strength to be alarmed. I may have covered my face with my hands; I think I remember the vanilla perfume I'd used for the first time that morning, the scent of which was still on my hands. I don't remember if I cried, but for two days I couldn't speak a single word.

New York, 29 September 2000

I went to see the lawyer this morning. He had me sign the papers for selling the gallery. As he handed me the file, he smiled at me. "That's a tidy sum of money. What will you do with it all?" He was a friend of my father's; I didn't want to lie to him so I told him that I might buy an apartment in Paris, that I might do some travelling in Europe and maybe, who knows, in Asia . . . He must have sensed that I was a little lost, that I had no real plans. As I was leaving he put his hand on my shoulder and told me solemnly, in a near-whisper, "You know, Judith, if you ever need help or advice, don't hesitate . . ." I didn't reply. But long after leaving his office, that remark kept running through my head, like a gentle, reassuring song.

*

The following year, Antoine and Séverine didn't see much of each other. Back in Paris, Antoine often thought about the time they'd spent together in Cork, perhaps accomplishing in dreams what he'd lacked the boldness to try in reality. Ironically, Séverine seemed to him even more accessible now that he no longer saw her every day, and when he came home from the lycée, exhausted, in search of a small diversion before he went back to studying, it was always the memory of Séverine that came to mind. She occupied an indefinite space, a place that he'd imagined belonged to him but that he'd not yet taken the trouble to explore. She was a vague and enigmatic presence who made him think, maybe we could be together, just not right now.

They weren't in touch for a few months. Then, at Christmas, Antoine received a card: "Dear Antoine, I hope that 1991 will bring you much success and happiness. All good wishes, Séverine." That card, coming after several months of silence, puzzled him. He didn't want to admit that he was disappointed; it would have meant acknowledging that he'd been expecting of her feelings that he wasn't sure he had himself. But something about the card irritated him, he couldn't really say what. Maybe it was the neutral, indifferent tone, probably the one she'd adopted for all the other cards she sent.

Several times in the weeks to come Antoine thought about Séverine's card. He told himself that he must reply to it, and that thought alone kept Séverine present in his memory. But he couldn't decide if he should send a card or a letter—or what he should write. Repeat the same trivial clichés? Or pour his heart out, tell her whatever came into his mind? None of those solutions seemed appropriate. He hesitated, days passed, then weeks, and when it was February, Antoine started to tell himself that it didn't make much sense to send her a Christmas card and that it would probably be better to phone her. One night he looked for her number, and not finding it after looking for an hour, he gave up. Surely she would call him eventually.

She didn't. For lack of time, perhaps—final exams were approaching and she didn't want to let herself be distracted—or perhaps from apprehension too, because she wasn't sure of his feelings for her and didn't want to encourage him to think she saw him as someone other than a friend.

*

New York, 6 October 2000

When I was a little girl I was very superstitious. No, I wasn't afraid to walk under a ladder or to cross paths with a black cat; I was fairly indifferent to that sort of thing. But I had composed my own world of rules and prohibitions. When I ate a peach or a plum, for instance, and my teeth accidentally touched the pit, I was sure it would bring me bad luck. When I switched off the light before I fell asleep at night, I had to be careful to touch the switch only with my index finger. If I inadvertently used my middle finger or my thumb, I had to switch it back on, count to a hundred and switch it off again. It all seems ridiculous today; I can't imagine where those weird ideas came from and how they could have had such a hold over me. Perhaps the world around me was so poor, so bland, so bereft of powerful emotions—or maybe I myself was so avid to create some—that I was seeking by every means to fill it with omens and meanings that only I could understand and that I didn't try to share.

    For some weeks, all sorts of memories began to surface. It was my father's death, most likely, but there was also the fact that I'd come to a time in my life, perhaps, when the past had become so heavy that I was forced to focus on it. When Dad referred to silly things I'd done when I was six, my fascination with animals or my talent for drawing, I listened indifferently. Now, I am hungry for his stories. I'd have liked him to tell me about the games he played with me when I was a baby, what he did to make me laugh. At night, when I can't get to sleep, I turn the same old memories over and over in my head, hoping that they will lead me to others, hidden away deep in my mind. It seems to me that those lost memories would help me to understand what I've become and to reshape my life. But memories don't change a life. And if today I take such pleasure in turning the past over and over, it is not only because I've accumulated baggage that is beginning to weigh on me. It is also, perhaps, because I can no longer see what the future might have in store, and because, if I have no plans, it's in my memory that I should seek out new directions for my life.

*

Antoine and Séverine would most likely have forgotten one another, and the weeks they'd spent in Cork would have melted bit by bit into the vague mass of memories they no longer had any use for if, one week after graduation, they hadn't met by chance on the terrace of the Café Rostand across from the Jardin du Luxembourg. Antoine was coming back from the banks of the Seine, his knapsack crammed with books he'd bought at stalls along the quays, and Séverine was having lunch with her father, who worked nearby. When she saw Antoine coming up to their table, Séverine stood, kissed his cheeks as if she weren't surprised at all to see him and, somewhat ill at ease, introduced him to her father, a pot-bellied man with heavy eyebrows and piercing eyes. He turned off his scowl just long enough for a brief smile and then, ignoring them both, as if he were trying to show them that he had no interest in their secrets, immediately sat down again and went on eating, eyes focused on his plate. Antoine had no time to pay attention to him. To hide her nervousness, Séverine was bombarding him with questions: How had his exams gone? What were his plans for next year? Where was he spending his holidays? When Antoine told her that he would spend the summer working in his uncle's restaurant in Antibes,

Séverine couldn't contain her surprise and, for a moment, seemed to have regained a little spontaneity: she was spending her holidays in the south of France too, in Cannes, where her mother had an apartment. Antoine should have shown more enthusiasm, but he was so sure nothing would happen between him and Séverine that the prospect of seeing her in Cannes left him a little flustered. And so he just smiled dreamily. "What a coincidence... we should try to get together..." They exchanged phone numbers and, out of courtesy rather than to please him, Antoine bade Séverine's father a ceremonious goodbye. Still busy with his steak, the man gave him a quick glance that seemed to say, "I'm well aware of your intentions, young man. And you'd be well advised to leave my daughter alone; she's worth a hundred times more than you."

*

Antoine's uncle had a pizzeria outside Antibes. Very popular with tourists—especially Americans and Germans—it had a certain appeal to the local population too, despite its stucco walls and the operetta music played there from morning till night. Antoine, whose uncle had offered him the job so that he could spend his holiday on the Côte while he earned a little money, hadn't expected to work so hard. His days began around ten-thirty a.m. to prepare for opening and often didn't end till after midnight. He had two days off, Sunday and Monday, and his salary was the same as that of the other employees. It didn't take Antoine long to realize that he wasn't cut out to be a waiter—he was awkward, half the time he made mistakes when taking orders and he seemed incapable of bringing the food on time. Mornings, he was too exhausted to go out and though he didn't like to sleep in, he had to stay in bed to recover. He was determined not to give up though. He had a vague hope that things might improve and he didn't want to let his uncle down.

The first three nights, despite his exhaustion, Antoine stayed for a while after closing, chatting with one of the waitresses, a young woman his age. She had a broad, mild-looking face, a small pug nose that didn't seem to belong to her and hair dyed such a vivid red that she appeared to be wearing a wig. She smiled a lot and her big green eyes seemed frozen in a surprisingly happy expression.

Sitting at a table near the bar they talked quietly over a cognac. The young woman—her name was Julie—was enrolled in art history at the University of Nice. She lived alone with her mother and in the summer worked to pay for her education. As he didn't feel like talking about himself, Antoine encouraged her to go on, asking her about Nice, the university, her courses. On the third night, Julie had alluded to a boy she'd met at university the year before. She hadn't referred to him as her "boyfriend," but from the way she talked about him Antoine had sensed that she thought of him as more than a mere friend—even if it wasn't necessarily mutual. Antoine tried to imagine her in love—her blurred features suddenly precise, her soft lips strained in the expectation of a tender remark, the expression of perpetual astonishment in her gaze finally filled with meaning. He thought to himself that there must be a way to see her as beautiful—or at the very least pretty—and as an exercise in mental conversion, did his best to find out what about her could arouse desire. Yes, her hips were too broad; yes, her expression was to say the least disconcerting—in the dim light, it was even alarming, like a hysterical, desperate cry for help—yes, her heavy legs evoked only pure thoughts: you might have wanted to paint them, but not to touch them. And yet, thought Antoine, her skin looked soft, as soft as the breeze. Her smile was filled with tenderness, without a hint of an ulterior motive, a smile that held nothing back and was held back by nothing. And wasn't there a certain grace in her too-heavy body? Perhaps the sight of her naked would offer to the eyes rewards that her appearance kept one from imagining.

Antoine tried so hard to think of the angle that could make the young woman seem attractive that he couldn't imagine she might be attracted to him. If he had, it might have been enough to make him see her as beautiful. But he was eager for just one thing: sleep; and when she suggested that he come with her and a group of friends on a boat ride the following Sunday, Antoine refused politely, pleading a visit to friends that day.

It may have been to add a bit of truth to the lie that he finally decided to call Séverine the next day. He hadn't wanted to when he arrived, lest he seem overly enthusiastic, but now he was impatient to see her, to escape, even for just a few hours, the boredom of his job. They arranged to meet in a crêperie near the port.

*

Antoine turned up at the crêperie the following Sunday around half-past eleven. Séverine, who'd been waiting for a while, had her nose in a book, which she stuffed into her purse when she spotted him. She seemed different, not as anxious as the last time he'd seen her, in Paris.

Antoine sat down and immediately started talking about himself, his job at the pizzeria, his plans. Séverine did the same, a little too feverishly perhaps—her degree, the days at a time spent reviewing material, the fear of failing, and finally the relief, the pleasure at having nothing to do for one whole summer. Both made tremendous efforts to appear interested in what the other was saying. It was as if they were competing to fill the silence with words, to leave no lull in the conversation. And then, suddenly, as if she had prepared ages ago and couldn't wait to tell him, Séverine announced that she'd met someone, a guy named Patrick, two months before the end of the school year. He wasn't in the same class, but they often met when they were leaving the school, and since he lived close to her, they sometimes went home together at night. He had taken an internship at a bank in Paris but would come to visit her at the end of the month. From her sparkling eyes, from her restrained smile, Antoine could see that Séverine really had changed. When she said shyly, like a child owning up to stealing a candy, that she couldn't wait to see him, that she missed him, that she couldn't stop thinking about him, Antoine knew she was sincere.

He should have been happy for her—and he did his best to appear so, asking questions about Patrick, his courses, his plans. But at the same time he felt betrayed, not because of his feelings for her—he himself was unsure and preferred, even when he was alone, to dodge the question—but because of the contrite, nearly guilty manner she'd adopted, as if it were obvious that she was going to hurt him.

*

New York, 24 October 2000

David called this afternoon. When I heard his voice I couldn't hide my surprise. I never thought I'd hear from him again. When I told him I'd decided to go back to Paris, he insisted on coming to see me.

He was late, as usual. Before sitting down he walked around the living room, glancing at books on the table, turning his gaze to the window, watching people walking by on Houston Street. As he wasn't sure what to say and sensed that I was going to remain silent, he started talking about himself. He didn't take his eyes off me, as if my slightest reaction mattered more than what he was saying. He explained that he'd become an interior decorator, refurbishing the apartments of wealthy New York bankers. He was trying to justify giving up painting and wanted to convince me that he was totally satisfied with his life.

While appearing to listen I watched him fiddle with a pencil he'd taken out of his pocket. I remembered how expressive his hands had seemed the first time we met. I thought to myself that such sensual hands could only belong to someone who was capable of great things. And then of course I realized that I'd been wrong. He reminded me a little of a cat: behind the grace and nobility of his movements, nothing but silence and the peaceful void of the eternal present.

That's also why I was never in love with David. Not just because I wasn't ready or was afraid of having to live through another heartbreak. No, it's because it was impossible to experience powerful feelings for David. Even with just the two of us together he seemed distant. At first I thought he was running away, that he had something to hide. I told myself there must have been some tragic event in his life and that he was trying to avoid any conversation that in any way whatsoever might revive the memory. But he'd had an uneventful childhood, his parents were still alive and he seemed to be surrounded by people who loved him. I think he gave the impression of running away because he wasn't in the habit of looking inside himself. Some people are absent because they're elsewhere. David was absent because he was nowhere. Had he searched inside himself he'd probably have found nothing frightening, nothing that could have stirred pity or disgust—and that may have been the very thing that drove him away from himself and made him seem evasive.

What was great about David was that no questions were asked. He would come by the gallery to pick me up, we'd have dinner in Chinatown or SoHo and spend the night together, sometimes at my apartment, most often at his. We didn't need to talk. We would undress hastily and slip between the sheets, almost without looking at one another. Our faces barely touched.

It was all very simple: he didn't love me and I didn't love him either. I can't even claim that I loved his body. When you love someone's body you love them entirely. I loved small pieces of David: the hair but not the nose, the stomach but not the arms, the mouth but not the eyes. In fact, it was precisely because I didn't love David that he could give me so much pleasure. When we love, our expectations of pleasure are too high. We want it to live up to our love. We don't see that pleasure is selfish, that it drives us away from the other.

David had stopped talking, having run out of things to say about himself and preferring an uncomfortable silence to my bored expression. "What about you, what are your plans?" I finally decided to answer his questions. I told him about my father's death, the funeral, the sale of the gallery. And as I had nothing to prove to him, I told him the truth: I didn't really have any plans.

He got up to go to the bathroom. Out of the corner of my eye I saw him glance furtively around my bedroom. I thought I saw him smile. Maybe he was curious to know if there was a man in my life; not necessarily out of jealousy but out of a sort of professional interest, a little like a doctor who follows from a distance the progress of a former patient and wants to be sure that she's in good hands.

I went to the kitchen to rinse the glasses. Standing at the sink I heard him approach. I felt his hand on my shoulder. For a moment, I thought he was going to kiss me and I was already prepared to push him away, but he simply took my hands and told me, squeezing them and struggling to look sincere, "Well, good luck!" There was a bit of pity in his expression, as if he were reassured to note that I wasn't happy without him.

New York, 25 October 2000

I reread what I wrote yesterday. I don't know why I started talking about David. I won't miss him. If he died tomorrow I wouldn't feel the least bit sad. The one who does matter I've hardly mentioned. I don't really feel like talking about him. I wouldn't know how to do it, where to begin.

Just two more days.

*

Over the following weeks Antoine and Séverine saw more of each other. On his days off Antoine would set out for Cannes in the morning and on weeknights, he would borrow his uncle's moped to go and meet Séverine in Antibes or Juan-les-Pins. They liked to walk along the beach in the evening and look at the displays of candies, the cheap jewellery, the chrome sunglasses. They lingered in front of the paintings exhibited under the streetlamps, the photos of sunsets, the caricatures of movie stars. Sometimes an artist sitting on a makeshift bench, mistaking them for lovers, would suggest doing their portrait. They didn't mind being taken for a couple. On the contrary, when a merchant gave them a wink or a waitress offered them a table in a quiet corner, "away from the crowd," they smiled and exchanged a knowing look. The gaze of others made their relationship seem nearly illicit, not because they were secretly in love but, on the contrary, because they gave the impression of being in love even though they weren't. Their secret was that they didn't love one another, and that secret brought them closer.

    This paradoxical intimacy freed Antoine from the unfinished dreams that had taken root in him when they met in Cork. For the first time, he realized that what they had was far more precious than whatever it is that binds lovers: the certainty, invisible to others, that their relationship would live on forever in the vicinity of love. Saving themselves, safeguarding themselves in that way, had let them create a space that belonged to them more intimately than the place of desire that all couples share. As for Séverine, she too felt liberated. First because she no longer had to worry about fending off Antoine's advances—even the most implicit. And then because, thanks to Antoine, she still had the leisure to think that she was free and unattached. He was for her the person who kept open the road to all possibilities, the living symbol of all the encounters, all the adventures that still awaited her. Perhaps.

*

Sunday afternoons, Séverine usually looked after her sister's children. Antoine would join her after lunch and they'd all go to the beach together. Antoine helped the eldest, Sébastien, build sand castles, while the boy's two little sisters went with Séverine to look for shells. One night they had taken the children for a walk along the Croisette before going home for dinner. Each of them took one of Sophie's, the youngest child's, hands and pulled her arms up to make her jump. Antoine looked at Séverine's hand clasping the little girl's. For him to be holding Sophie's other hand struck him as nearly indiscreet, as if, indirectly, it was Séverine's. This contact by proxy reminded him that, not so long ago, Séverine had still been the object onto which he'd projected a vague hope, an image—still hazy and nameless—of an imaginary alliance. They were only friends, but friends on whom the memory of a possibility greater than friendship had been sealed, the memory of a boundless life, with no edges or duration, that would always, despite their efforts, be with them. From the corner of his eye he observed Séverine, who was totally occupied with amusing the little girl. Behind that perfect indifference, though, it struck him as unbelievable that Séverine too did not feel touched—or at the very least brushed—by that clandestine contact.

*

New York, 26 October 2000

I went to the graveyard this morning. One of the guards very kindly explained to me at length how to find my father's grave. He even gave me a map. I got lost anyway though. It was a fine day, I wasn't in a hurry, so I walked for a while. Practically everyone I saw was an old lady. I watched them come and go, muffled in their fur coats. They pulled out weeds, snipped wilted flowers, laid fresh bouquets. Walking by them, I looked at the names on the tombstones. In most cases it was probably a husband, a parent. I thought to myself that after I left, there would be no one to tend my father's grave.

I kept walking, vaguely looking for the entrance to the cemetery. That was when I found Dad's grave, at the end of a path lined with maples.

I wasn't too sure what to do next. I've never known how to pray and I hadn't brought flowers. I told myself that probably the best thing to do was to call up happy moments with Dad: vacations by the sea, walks in Vincennes or the Bois de Boulogne, restaurant dinners on Saturday night. But in all those memories Mom was present too, and Dad, as usual, was completely absorbed in her. Then, suddenly, a different memory—come from I don't know where: a winter afternoon, I must have been eight or nine, and Dad had come to pick me up at school. It was the last thing I expected, usually Mom picked me up and generally I only saw Dad at night, before I went to bed. Something must have come up to keep Mom away—maybe she'd gone to see her brother, who was beginning to be sick at the time—and Dad had taken the day off to be with me. He took me to an Italian restaurant near his office on place de Breteuil. I remember that he'd let me order a Coke, something Mom never allowed. I drank it very slowly, in tiny sips, so it would last till the end of the meal. I also remember an aquarium filled with crayfish and lobsters. I was fascinated by their tiny, fierce heads and their black eyes that seemed to follow my own. In one corner of the aquarium there was a lobster missing a claw and I asked Dad how he'd lost it. He explained that probably it had happened during a fight with another, stronger lobster. And anticipating my next question, he added that male lobsters fight to win over the females. I asked if it was the same for humans and his reply, which I remember, puzzled me. "Yes, it's nearly the same with men, except that usually we don't fight physically. Instead we try to prove that we're smarter, wealthier or more talented than the others." To which I responded, "I wouldn't want boys to fight over me; I'd rather be the one fighting over them." Dad must have been struck by my reaction because he liked talking about it. Over the years, in fact, his impressions were probably superimposed on mine, so much so that I'm not even sure it's a real memory. But it doesn't matter. What matters is that Dad himself remembered the restaurant dinner and that he talked about it so often.

Climbing out of the subway, I bought myself a pretzel and a can of Coke. I didn't feel like going straight home so I went walking in Central Park. In spite of the cold, the, park was full of young men on in-line skates, zipping past the men and women out for a stroll. Elegant women wrapped in fur coats walked briskly, cellphones stuck to their ears. I tried to catch bits of their conversations—detailed instructions to the nanny, swapping gossip with friends, making dates with lovers or husbands. There was something about this frenzied activity that attracted me. These women never stopped to catch their breath, but everything they did had a precise goal, an assigned spot in a coherent whole. The only questions they asked were logistical: What time should I come for my yoga lesson? Where can I get my little girl's ballet shoes? What caterer should I use for the party on Saturday? I imagine all this fuss is reassuring; after all, for each of these questions there is generally only one correct answer. At the end of the day these women must feel they've accomplished everything they needed to, and that now they can close their eyes and say to themselves, "Yes, really, everything was in its place today." As for me, when I finally go to bed late into the night, all I think about is what I could have done and I wonder why, once again, I was so lacking in courage.

I sat on a park bench and took my Coke out of my bag. As I opened it, I remembered what Dad had said to me when we came home from the restaurant that time he picked me up at school: "Don't tell your mother that I let you order a Coke. It will be our secret, all right?"

*

Summer was nearly over. On the last weekend Séverine and Antoine had decided to stroll around Antibes. The air was heavy and the streets of the old town, overrun with tourists, had lost the peaceful charm that made them so attractive during the day. They made their way to the seaside in search of some peace and quiet. Their walk brought them to the lighthouse. Leaning on the low wall they looked at the harbour lights dancing on the waves. Now the silence did not make Antoine uncomfortable. Not because he'd exhausted every topic of conversation. On the contrary, it was because he still had so much to say to her that he no longer felt the need to talk.

Antoine and Séverine had learned how to avoid the deeds and words that would have brought them too close together. And since, within the limits imposed on them, their feelings kept coming back to the same familiar words, the silence had acquired the power to open up unknown perspectives, a space in which their uncertainties could move more freely than within the constraint of words. In silence, Antoine thought to himself, they were free to imagine the other's love without having to acknowledge it.

Suddenly, a voice drew Antoine from his musing. "Antoine! What are you doing here?" A young woman in a bathing suit was standing behind them, arms akimbo. Her hair, swept by the wind, half-hid her face. It was only when he noticed her bulging eyes, frozen in astonishment, that he recognized Julie, the waitress in his uncle's restaurant. He introduced her to Séverine, who gazed at her, intrigued. Antoine, obviously ill at ease, would have liked to cut short the conversation. But Julie, apparently not understanding, went on asking him questions. Antoine felt Séverine's eyes on him, inquiring, "Who's this girl who seems to know you so well? When did you meet? Why have you never mentioned her?"

In fact, Séverine would never have asked such questions. But Antoine thought that if he'd been in her shoes he might have asked them himself, and that was all it took to make Julie's presence unbearable. Then something strange happened: he took Séverine's hand and, explaining to Julie that they were meeting some friends, he turned his back, leading Séverine away with him. He had taken her hand so firmly and confidently that it never occurred to Séverine to resist and it wasn't until long afterwards, when they were walking back, that their hands separated.

Antoine tried to explain to Séverine who Julie was, but she didn't seem interested. Antoine imagined that, because of his embarrassed manner, Séverine might think that he and Julie had slept together, and that it was in a spirit of possessiveness—to make Julie understand that Antoine didn't belong to her—that Séverine had let him take her hand. Or perhaps Séverine felt that Antoine wanted to prove to the young waitress that he wasn't interested in her and that he was, so to speak, "already taken." For Séverine, though, the act simply summed up her feelings for Antoine: he was the final limit, the ultimate barrier that she could get close to but mustn't cross. Giving him her hand was a declaration that there would never be a kiss. It meant recognizing that their feelings, of which they'd only allowed themselves to see the surface, would not have the upper hand, that they would be forever like those nostalgic tunes we avoid listening to too often because we're afraid of the imperfectly forgotten memories they're likely to bring back.

2

Chelsea, London, 17 March 2002

One a.m. Lying on her back staring at the ceiling, Madeleine Labée can't get back to sleep. She tries to convince herself that it's already five or six o'clock, but she knows that it's much earlier and that sleep will not return. Every night it's the same thing. Her doctor has prescribed pills, but she's reluctant to take them. She doesn't want to drag herself around the house half-asleep all day, unable to work up the energy to go out. As she does every night, she fixes herself a tisane with honey, more out of habit than in the hope that it will help her get back to sleep. She's tried everything: homeopathy, yoga, hot baths, breathing exercises. Nothing works. When she was little and couldn't sleep, her mother would tell her to clear her mind. Today she still tries to get rid of her preoccupations, to silence the thoughts that are disturbing her, but actually there are so few that she wonders if they really are the cause of her insomnia. She has the normal cares of a normal person: wonders when the plumber will come to fix the toilet, mustn't forget to return the books to the library, hopes that spring won't be too rainy. That's not what keeps you from sleeping.

There's also Raoul. Ever since he started sharpening his claws on the living-room carpet she's had to resign herself to letting him go out. It was the veterinarian who recommended it: "Raoul is a male, Madame Labée. Even though he's castrated he needs to go outside and let off steam. If you won't let him, he'll start to urinate in your houseplants, he'll shred your curtains, scratch your furniture..." Now that he was free to go outside whenever he wanted he did seem calmer. But she was constantly afraid that he'd be run over by a car. It had happened to her neighbour's cat last summer. A reckless driver, apparently, who enjoyed running over anything that was in his way. Now whenever Madeleine hears a car go by she worries—"I hope Raoul's not on the street, I hope it isn't that reckless driver who kills cats"—and when she hears him scratch at the kitchen window, she hurries to let him in, takes him in her arms, kisses him all over. Madeleine can imagine what the neighbours say behind her back: "Poor thing, she's demented. Never got over her husband's death. She's absolutely enamoured of that horrible cat. Really, it's pathetic." But Madeleine doesn't pay too much attention to them. Let them think what they want. She knows what it's like to love and be loved by a cat...

Suddenly she hears tires screech on the street, then a muffled sound. She immediately thinks, Raoul! She jumps out of bed and races to the window, makes out a car that has stopped, headlights off, at the corner of Flood Street. Madeleine puts on her dressing gown and hurtles down the stairs. She thinks to herself: "Let it not be that damn reckless driver . . . I hope nothing's happened to Raoul . . ." Just as she is opening the front door she hears the car start. She runs to the place where it had stopped. There, in the light of the streetlamp, she sees a woman stretched out on the pavement, the contents of her purse scattered around her. Madeleine can't hold back a sigh of relief. She looks around: not a sound; the street is deserted. Suddenly she jumps: something rubs against her legs. Raoul! She takes him in her arms. "Raoul, my darling cat, it's you . . . I was so frightened, if you only knew . . . so frightened . . ." The cat rubs his head against Madeleine's face. He licks her tears, purring. A few moments later Madeleine comes back to herself.

"Come with me, my love. We're going home. We have to call the police."

*

Paris, 15 November 2000

I've reread what I wrote before leaving New York and don't exactly know how to pick up the thread.

Somewhat nostalgically, I think back to my final days in New York. My life was totally empty, as empty as it is now, but maybe precisely because I had nothing to fill it with, I felt strangely free. I could let myself go, stroll through museums, spend hours in front of my little TV and not have to tell myself I was wasting my time. I could savour fully, without the slightest guilt, each futile moment, because I was living the final moments of an existence that I'd chosen to leave, that no longer had any attraction for me.

There is also the fact that when I think back to my life in New York, my memory, like a negative image, settles only on what I currently miss. And now I feel only the anxiety of a life on hold, with no schedule, no pressure, no direction. That carefree life, which had seemed so seductive when I was getting ready to leave New York, now feels like a burden. I need something to do that will fill my days and keep me away from myself. I need discipline. I need most of all to no longer be alone.

*

The weeks after their return to Paris, Antoine and Séverine spoke on the phone several times. Antoine tried to entertain her by talking about his problems with the university administration and describing the eccentricities of his professors in the Mathematics Department. Séverine too spoke about her studies, her law courses, the "inhuman amount" of information she had to take in every week. Sometimes she mentioned Patrick, who'd found a job with an insurance company. Antoine didn't ask any questions about him, afraid of seeming too indifferent or not indifferent enough. Nor did he talk about their holidays the past summer, about their strolls along the seaside in Cannes and Antibes. What was there to say? Those moments were lodged in their memories. To summon them now wouldn't have brought them closer. It might even have driven them apart; they'd have felt more keenly how far removed their lives were from that time. They would have remembered the landscapes, the places they'd visited together, but they wouldn't have recovered their feelings. It was as if they'd been put away in a separate, less accessible part of their memories that could be reached only at the cost of extraordinary concessions. And their memories would have filed before their eyes, divided, devoid of life and taste, like a film with the sound cut.

*

Paris, 28 November 2000

I finally moved into a small apartment on rue Keller, close to the Bastille. At first I looked in familiar neighbourhoods, near the Place d'Italie where I spent my childhood, and in the 15th where I was living before I left Paris. I even visited a studio in the building where we'd lived before moving to boulevard Raspail. But memories quickly lose their charm and I'm sure I would have felt stifled by those places that would have been constant reminders of my childhood. It's not good to live surrounded by memories, especially if you're alone.

And if you want to safeguard your memories, you mustn't go back too often to places where you've lived and, even more, you mustn't settle down there. At first, everything takes you back to the past: the smell of wax in the building staircase, the door that slams as it shuts behind you, the echo of your footsteps in the dark corridor. But repetitions make these impressions detach themselves from the past. Blended into everyday life, eventually they would erode and no longer remind us of anything. Like a piece of music you've listened to over and over, until the emotion has become impervious. If we want our memories to retain a little of their magic, we must learn to evoke them in moderation.

*

Yesterday morning when I was walking near the Panthéon, I noticed an ad in the window of a small antiquarian bookstore. They were looking for a "saleswoman with experience and, ideally, knowledgeable about modern art." I left my CV, just in case. At all costs, I must keep busy.

*

Over the following months, Antoine and Séverine got together regularly. They sometimes met for breakfast in a café on boulevard Saint-Michel or strolled in the Jardin du Luxembourg at lunchtime. Now and then Séverine would talk about Patrick, his courses, the films they'd seen together. She talked about him in a way that was a little remote, as if he were some vague acquaintance or a distant cousin. But maybe for that very reason, Antoine felt that a routine must have settled into their lives. He understood from her silences, her omissions, that it had become impossible for her to imagine her life without Patrick. Antoine, though, was less circumspect about his own private life. He found Séverine to be a patient and generous confidant. When he explained that he couldn't feel anything at all for the girls he met, when he talked with the greatest detachment about his latest breakup, Séverine listened without judging him. She asked questions, tried to understand. Most of all she tried to instill confidence in him. He would meet someone who'd change all that, she was sure of it. It would take patience and he mustn't try too hard. "You'll see. It will happen when you least expect it." In the end, this blind optimism reassured him. Maybe because Séverine seemed so happy, he told himself that she must be right. Maybe too because he sensed that she wanted his happiness more sincerely, more fully than she would have if they'd allowed love to grow between them.

*

Paris, 12 December 2000

I remember reading in my childhood room, the sunlight on the corner of my desk, the chalky smell of the books in the Pléaide collection—and none of that will ever be able to give life to those memories or to bring me closer to them. Everything I can imagine today, my thoughts, what I translate into words, is already another memory, other smells, another light, frozen in a consciousness that is no longer mine.

Paris, 4 January 2001

I have been gone for nine years now, nine years that I've spent trying to forget Antoine.

 And yet I keep telling myself that I loved him as I've never loved anyone else, as I will never be able to love again. And I tell myself that no one has loved me or will ever be able to love me as he did. I have to admit, though, that there's probably as much illusion as truth in all of that. Had we not been separated, had we, like so many others, experienced love as part of everyday life, we surely would have ended up hating each other—or we would have resigned ourselves to a monotonous life, without contrast, in which only the memory of the first moments would have kept us together. And I'm not even certain what my feelings for him were. The breakup deposited a heavy layer of sediment—the pain of no longer having him, the loneliness that followed the separation, the lack of passion for the men I'd met after him—that made the memories inaccessible to me. I'm in love with him today as I perhaps would never have been if we hadn't separated. I love him with all my love but also, above all, with all his absence, all my loneliness, all the vulnerability of my memories. I love him because the absence of the loved one, because of the void it leaves in us, can easily become the entire universe.

Paris, 6 January 2001

If Antoine and I had had time to get used to one another, I probably wouldn't think about him now with such passion. It would have been the same love, but spread over a longer period, watered down into confident words, into impulses blunted by too much certainty. Our affection—no longer an apparition but the familiar response to a familiar hope, spread into all the cracks in everyday life—would have brought us nothing but comfort and not the remarkable surprise of belonging to one another. Each new gesture would have been the memory of someone else, his smile, identical to a thousand ancient smiles; I would have imagined it, I would have expected it, it would come not from him but from my own consciousness. It was in the risk of losing him, of not yet having him, that I realized how much I needed him. My head is still full of all the moments that we did not live, and my memory of those few months spent together contains in itself as much desire as a lifetime's worth of love.

Paris, 7 January 2001

It's the loves we haven't lived that are the hardest to forget.

*

It was in the month of June 1991. Sitting at the back of the room, a snifter of cognac in his hand, Antoine was watching the couples dance. In the church, earlier, he had settled in the last row, as if he were not a guest but a stranger. When Séverine had told him she was going to marry Patrick, Antoine had been only half-surprised. For some time he had suspected that the moment would come, but he hadn't tried to prepare himself. Séverine, very excited, had explained to him that Patrick had got down on his knees to ask for her hand and Antoine, so as not to let her down, had done his best to seem enthusiastic and congratulated her effusively.

During the ceremony he had thought Séverine was dazzling. In a tight-waisted white silk gown she seemed taller than usual. She had the same generous and confident smile for all the guests. One's gaze no longer stopped on her large nose, her fine pale lips, her somewhat angular hips. One saw only the grace of her movements, the tenderness in her eyes. At the altar she stood very erect, chin high, bosom slightly rounded, like a statue that had suddenly come to life. She resembled the noble and passionate women in Renaissance paintings, so beautiful that no one dares to desire them.

During the reception, Séverine introduced Antoine to her friends from law school. From their questions he realized that Séverine had never mentioned him—he was a friend among others, but one who was a stranger. He filled a very small part of Séverine's life, isolated from the rest, like a remote island that she sometimes visited in secret and never mentioned to the others.

At dinner, Antoine was seated next to one of Séverine's cousins. She lived in Nantes and as her husband travelled a lot, he hadn't been able to accompany her. She probably would have liked Antoine to show more interest in her, maybe even hoped, without altogether admitting it, for some flirting. But Antoine was too tired to make the effort to please her—and in any case his mind was elsewhere. When the guests got up to dance after the dessert, Antoine stayed by himself.

Staring into space, he watched as couples came together for a dance and then drifted apart. He wondered how long these men and women would stay together, what disappointments, what betrayals stood out already in their future. He tried to imagine their first meeting, their first looks—still hesitant, still ambiguous. Their smiles were only questions and didn't expect an answer. His daydream took him back to the moments he and Séverine had spent together in Cork, a few years earlier. If he had been able to see Séverine as he saw her now, his life might have taken a different turn. He would have made the first move, she might not have pushed him away, and the following summer in Cannes, who knows... Antoine tried to recall his state of mind when he was in Cork. He remembered his stupid obsession with girls who weren't interested in him, who weren't even aware that he existed. And while he was getting lost in futile hopes, Séverine had been there, maybe just waiting for a move from him. His exhausted and feverish memory then invented new recollections: of himself and Séverine walking along the River Lee. On the way home Antoine finally decided, after endless hesitations, to take her hand, and in the wan light of the streetlamps, they kissed, leaning against a railing. To complete his dream, the bells of a distant church rang for vespers, as if to announce that the spell was broken, that another life—all the more solid and tangible because it had been put off for so long—could finally begin.

Intoxication was creeping over him and Antoine, exhausted, was about to leave when he saw Séverine, light and smiling, coming up to his table. She sat down next to him without a word. Patrick was on the other side of the room, talking with friends, and only a few couples were still dancing. Séverine gazed at Antoine with her big brown eyes, as if she were expecting him to question her. "I'm very glad you came," she said finally. "I hope you weren't too bored."

"No, no, on the contrary." He looked at her intently, barely smiling. In the dim light her mouth seemed fuller, more determined. Her hair had come undone while she was dancing and a few black locks were stuck to her cheeks, making her face look whiter than usual. When Séverine smiled a small, half-moon shaped crease appeared above her mouth, like a second smile. Antoine hadn't noticed it before, and carried away, perhaps, by the sadness brought on by the wine, it seemed unbelievable to him that this small crease—the reflection, the joyous shadow of her smile—hadn't struck him before. A question popped into his mind, one that he was dying to ask Séverine: "If I'd tried to kiss you when we were in Cork would you have let me?" He was about to open his mouth when Séverine grabbed his arm and said, "Coming? Let's dance!" Although he hated to dance, Antoine let Séverine drag him onto the floor. The music was boisterous and Antoine couldn't follow it. Sometimes he stepped on Séverine's toes, sometimes he bumped into other couples, but Séverine seemed hardly aware. She was given over completely to the dance, unconcerned about the others, or about Antoine's discomfort and his awkwardness. She was content to look at him, smile at him, as if they were alone in this big room. At that moment Antoine felt, without understanding why, that Séverine was happy, happy to be dancing with him, and that nothing else mattered to her.

*

Paris, 27 January 2001

I've met someone. It will soon be three weeks. I haven't felt so light-hearted in a very long time.

Paris, 29 January 2001

He is so very thoughtful. Not just flowers, restaurants, phone calls at every hour of the day. It's also the way he looks at me, talks to me, touches me. I have the impression sometimes that I'm an immensely fragile person; he touches me as if he's afraid of breaking me.

The other night Alain and I didn't undress. I simply lay down on the bed. He pulled up my skirt and lay down on me. He started to kiss my face, my neck, my arms. And he spent a long time trying to enter me by thrusting against my tights. When he finally broke through them, my desire had gone but I was full of affection for him. The fact that he'd relinquished his own pleasure reassured me, as if he'd proven to me that I mattered to him, that he was there for me, and the rest was secondary. It may have been simply that the body's urge, when it lasts too long, eventually dissipates into affection and makes sexual pleasure pointless. But I wanted to convince myself that there was something else, that through his renunciation he was showing me his love. (Which proves that in spite of all my denials I have not completely lost the desire to be loved—even if it is by someone I'm not absolutely sure I love myself.)

*

Antoine and Séverine were sitting on a café terrace near the Madeleine. The sun warmed their faces; it was one of the last days of summer. They hadn't seen one another since the wedding three months earlier.

The conversation had got off to a slow, laborious start. Having asked Antoine some questions about the bank where he'd got a job as an analyst, Séverine started talking, without much enthusiasm, about her own work. Antoine looked at her face, fascinated to note how much it had changed in such a short time. She now wore a lot of makeup, her eyes seemed bigger, and her lips fuller. When she smiled, her teeth gleamed as if they belonged to a movie star. In her black pleated skirt, silk blouse and scarf knotted perfectly around her shoulders, she reminded him of the models in a fashion magazine, proud to be looked at, in particular proud of fitting in. Antoine imagined how much time Séverine must spend every morning getting ready and thought that all those efforts wiped out a little of her charm. But he was glad to be with her, reassured to sense that the bond between them had not been completely broken, that it lived on, transformed, and that without too much effort, they might be able to keep it from dying.

*

Paris, 2 February 2001

Three a.m. I can't get back to sleep. I can hear Alain snoring in the other bedroom. Mouth partly open, brows knit, as if he were desperately trying to remember something very simple; he's not very graceful when he sleeps. This is the first time he's stayed the night. He told his wife that he'd been sent to Madrid for the weekend.

I feel anxious, though we spent a wonderful evening. We'd arranged to meet in a café near the Odéon, then he took me to a small restaurant not far from my place. He insisted on ordering a bottle of red wine. Maybe he wanted to show me that he knew something about wine, maybe he thought I was a little sad and that a glass of wine would cheer me up—in any case, the wine soon went to my head and I must have said some very stupid things.

I told him about my life in New York, my work at the gallery and my father's death. I also told him that I'd started painting again and all at once he seemed very interested. He wanted to know what kind of paintings I did, whether I'd exhibited; he reproached me amiably for having never shown him my work. He too, apparently, had wanted to become an artist. During his university years he'd done a lot of drawing, mostly faces but also animals and battle scenes. It was, he said, a kind of obsession. He drew everywhere, on his notebooks, textbooks, newspapers. And at spare moments when he couldn't stand another word about the Civil Code and nothing would stay in his mind, he painted small pictures. Then, once his studies were over, he joined a law firm and that was the end. "Law and painting aren't a good fit, you know." Without much conviction I told him it was never too late, that he could always go back to it.

The candle on our table went out, filling the air with dense smoke. In the dim light his face seemed softer, almost vulnerable, as if he were certain that he'd won me over and was now waiting patiently until I asked him to take me home. And at that precise moment I told myself, he must be a poignant sight when he was asleep.

I can still hear him snoring, though not quite so loud. I hesitate to go back to my room, but I must try again to get back to sleep. I have to get up early tomorrow—I don't want to be late for work at the bookstore.

*

More than six months had passed since their last meeting. When she saw Antoine come in, Séverine nearly didn't recognize him. Pale, hollow-cheeked, his hair a mess, he looked as if he hadn't eaten for days. When she pecked his unshaven cheeks they prickled her face. He stared at her with bloodshot eyes as if she were an apparition, as if she were about to disappear.

The waiter came to their table and Antoine ordered a coffee without even looking at him.

"What's going on, Antoine?"

"I don't know... I don't know where to begin..."

He tried to smile but it looked more like a grimace.

"I've met someone... We were so happy, you can't imagine..."

"What happened?"

"I did something stupid... I was an idiot... It's all over now..."

By questioning him, Séverine was able to learn that her name was Judith, that she was a fine arts student and that she lived in the same building he did. They would see each other in the elevator now and then but it had taken Antoine months to work up the courage to speak to her. He had invited her for a coffee and they'd got together a few times for lunch.

"Sometimes," Antoine explained, "we'd go for a walk around the Jardin du Luxembourg. We talked a lot and that may be why it started slowly, as if we were trying to put off the moment... I don't know if I realized at the time how important she was to me—I didn't realize anything, the world around me had disappeared. I'd stopped questioning myself. There was only Judith, our long hours in bed, the pleasure of talking to her, of listening to her, of watching her sleep. It was as if all my dreams, all the stories that had nourished me on for years, had finally come true. I had nothing more to dream about, nothing more to desire. It lasted for six months and then..."

Antoine, whose face had relaxed a little when he was talking about Judith, darkened again. Séverine looked at him, motionless.

"Then what?" she asked hoarsely.

"I did something stupid. I don't know what came over me... One night Judith had gone home to study. Leaving the office, I ran into a colleague in the elevator. A girl of no interest, but pretty. I invited her for a drink, I don't know why. Maybe I suspected where it might lead, but I told myself that it was totally unimportant... In fact, I don't really know what I thought. Maybe I thought that if it came to that, I'd be able to resist, or else I convinced myself that it was all innocent... The truth is that I behaved like a son of a bitch. When I left her place it must have been three a.m. I'd had a fair amount to drink, but even though I was drunk I thought to myself, 'Judith must have called. She must have wondered why I wasn't there. She must have been worried.' After I got home, I didn't dare listen to my messages. I collapsed on my bed, promising myself that I'd wake up early and go to reassure her. The next morning it was she who woke me. It must have been eight or nine a.m. To explain the terrible shape I was in, I claimed that I'd gotten really drunk with a friend. She seemed to believe me. That might have been it, but over the next few days I couldn't stop thinking about what I'd done. Mentally, I repeated to myself the way the evening had passed, our encounter in the elevator, our conversation at the bar, our stroll down the Champs Élysées. I asked myself, 'Why did I offer to see her home? Why did I agree to go up with her? Why hadn't I left when there was still time?' I'd had so many opportunities to get a grip, to not get carried away. Even now, I can't understand. I wasn't even thinking about Judith. It was as if she didn't exist, as if she had never existed. I tormented myself like that for a week. Judith was well aware that something was wrong. I hardly talked to her any more. It's as if I were angry with her too. And I was, because she hadn't guessed, or if she had guessed, she'd said nothing, she'd behaved as if everything was the same, so that I went on bearing that unbearable secret by myself. I knew that I would hurt her if I told her what had happened. But I also told myself that none of it mattered, that she was the only one who mattered to me. And she would realize that there must be no secrets between us. She would perhaps realize what courage it had taken me to confess what I'd done and would find the strength to forgive me."

Séverine hadn't taken her eyes off Antoine's face. She could guess what would come next and she thought, "You shouldn't have said anything. There are things one must never say. You think you're safeguarding the integrity of what you have, but you're destroying it. You should have kept quiet and lived with your remorse, then you'd still be together today."

Antoine went on. "So one night I told her everything."

"What did she say?"

"Nothing. She didn't say a word. Didn't even cry. She simply turned over and went to sleep. I was relieved, my nightmare was finally over. In the days that followed, we didn't talk again about what had happened that night. Judith seemed more pensive than usual, but contrary to my fears, she wasn't hostile towards me at all—to the point that I really believed she'd forgiven me. Now, when I think back to that time, I realize there was something a little forced in her smiles, in her affectionate gestures. She wanted at all costs for me to believe that everything was as it had been before, that she wasn't angry with me. What she did, in fact, was numb my suspicions—the better to prepare for leaving. And what happened a week later did indeed take me completely by surprise. On Thursday I'd taken the train to London, where I had some business meetings. Judith and I had arranged to have lunch together when I came back on Saturday. But when I showed up at the bistro where we'd agreed to meet she wasn't there. After waiting for half an hour I phoned her, but there was no answer. Concerned, I went to her apartment; she wasn't there either. Her bedroom was untidier than usual; the drawers were open, her closet half-empty, her bed scattered with clothes, shoes, bottles of perfume and shampoo. I rushed to the concierge. She hadn't seen Judith that morning, but when she woke up she had found the key to her apartment under the door. I started to panic. Had she left a note, an address, a phone number to reach her? No. All she'd left was the key. The following days I forced myself to go to work. But I was only thinking about Judith. I tried to convince myself that she would come back. She had felt a need to go away for a few days, to get some distance. Maybe she'd gone to the country to spend a few days with friends? But time passed and I still had no news. It's been more than a month now; she definitely won't be coming back."

Séverine looked at Antoine, scrutinizing his face and dreading the moment when he would burst into tears. She wished she could reassure him. She wished she could tell him that after everything he and Judith had experienced together she would certainly come back. But Séverine didn't have the heart to lie to him.

"Did you try to get in touch with her friends, her professors, her classmates?"

"Of course. But no one knows anything."

"And her parents?"

"Her mother is dead and her father lives in the United States. In New York, I think."

Antoine had once again taken refuge in silence, a silence that meant there was nothing more to say, and most of all, that she shouldn't try to understand. Séverine sensed that nothing she might say would help Antoine. He himself had probably already nurtured all the vain hopes created by despair and any arguments she might come up with to convince him that all was not lost now seemed to her frivolous and pathetic.

Séverine tried to make eye contact with Antoine, but his eyes were focused on his cup, as if he were afraid of detecting on Séverine's face a trace of his own woes. Then Séverine brought her hands close to his and squeezed them hard, saying nothing.

*

Paris, 15 February 2001

I'd never have imagined an affair with a man like Alain. Not because he isn't my type—I've never dreamed of having any "type" in particular. Rather, I'm not at all drawn to his way of living. With David it was different. I wanted to belong to his world. I was attracted by the so-called bohemian existence he had created: the long evenings in a café with his university friends, his early-morning walks along the Hudson River (which was, he claimed, the source of his inspiration), his studio—"my pad," as he liked to call it when he wanted to sound like a Brit—with its dozens of half-finished paintings, old magazines and empty beer cans. There was, obviously, nothing natural about this meticulous disorder. Even his nonchalance had something premeditated about it. There was, though, something appealing and comforting about such a mastery of appearances, like a painting in which one would like to find oneself, where one could settle down peacefully, effortlessly, with no need to be concerned about existence.

Later, when I started dating Laurent, I also felt drawn by the world he moved in, by the image he projected of a man who devoted his entire life to a search for pleasure. It's true that in the beginning I found the diplomatic receptions deadly boring, but eventually

I got used to them. I enjoyed giving him a hand when he entertained at home. He explained to me at length the proper way to set the table, serve the soup, pour the wine—and I enjoyed following his instructions to the letter.

I also liked the almost ritual order he imposed on his life: jogging in Central Park every morning, his Alfa Romeo which he washed himself on Sunday afternoon, his Club Med vacations—always the same, near Syracuse in Sicily. What fascinated me above all was that he always seemed certain that he did things "properly." When he got dressed in the morning, he never hesitated over which tie or which shirt he should choose. And unlike many obsessives whose entire universe can be shaken by the discovery of a stain on their suit, Laurent never seemed bothered by anything at all.

Even—particularly—in love, there were elaborate rules to be respected. He would wash from head to toe before and after, and he expected me to do the same. There had to be candles in the bedroom and he always lit them himself. When I came to his place in the evening, a bottle of white wine and a bar of dark chocolate were waiting for us, to "awaken our senses." He also needed music and he chose the pieces with meticulous care. Physical love, he would say, was a "total experience," like opera, that required lengthy preparation and demanded total commitment. All that organization took a long time—and when Laurent was finally ready I was often fast asleep. But his love of setting the stage, his concern for the perfection of pleasure fascinated me. To him, everything was a matter of style. His life was like a baroque cathedral, filled with details and nooks and crannies, as if he took more satisfaction from interpreting his existence than from seizing moments of it.

With Alain, it's very different. His life, his work, what he does when we're not together—it all leaves me completely indifferent. Because he's married, of course, but also, I think, because I myself have changed. I no longer feel the urge to enter into the life of someone else. I'm not happy on my own, but I've also lost the certainty that everything would be sorted out if only I could dissolve into another universe.

Paris, 19 February 2001

Alain has theories about all kinds of things. It may be his lawyer's mind: everywhere, he tries to find the general rule. Last night he explained to me that in the body of any woman, even the ugliest, there is always a region capable of seducing, or at least of making a man dream: in one, it is the hollow at the nape of her neck, in another, the ear lobe, in yet another, a delicate wrist. If only those characteristics were the ones that desire usually seeks out, if only the eye were better trained to recognize their power to enchant, how many women seen as ugly would become the object of the most intense passions?

This morning I got up first. I took advantage of the time to tidy the kitchen a little. He woke up around seven and in no time at all he was ready to leave. What does he tell his wife when he spends the night with me? In the beginning I used to ask him; now I don't care. It's only one more lie and all his lies, in the end, resemble each other. He came up to me to say goodbye and I kept my back turned. I felt his hand alight on my shoulder and with the other, he lifted my hair to kiss the nape of my neck. I heard him take a long breath as if he wanted to take in the smell of my skin so that he could remember it later. I remembered what he'd said yesterday and I couldn't help wondering if, in his opinion, I belonged to the category of unappealing women in whom only a few regions ignored by other's gazes could, if discovered, become seductive. Maybe if he hadn't found my nape so pretty he would never have approached me. I didn't dare ask. I didn't want to hear him repeat that he found me beautiful, that he adored my body and so forth. I didn't want him to feel that I was vulnerable.

Paris, 21 February 2001

I dreamed about Dad last night. I was in a cemetery, looking for his grave. I'd been going in circles for hours. There wasn't a soul in the cemetery; I couldn't find anyone to ask for directions. Suddenly I felt a hand taking mine. I heard my father's grave and lilting voice: "Come here, I'll show you where it is." I didn't dare turn around to look at him—I was afraid he'd disappear. I allowed him to guide me down the shady paths in the graveyard. He was walking slowly, taking long strides. Now and then I heard him whistle. He appeared to be serene. While we were walking we began to play a game that I'd been very fond of in my childhood: he would squeeze my hand gently, two short, one long, or three longs followed by four shorts, and I had to repeat the same sequence exactly. It was our secret code, a code that seemed all the more precious to me because it didn't mean anything. The sequences became more and more complicated and when I made a mistake, he would merely smile and say, "All right, let's start again."

After walking for a long time we came to the end of a path lined with maples. His grave was there, bare and black. It was the only one not decorated with flowers. Finally, I turned towards Dad and abruptly pulled my hand away, stupefied: it was not my father, it was Antoine. He was looking at me tenderly, as if he were angry with himself for frightening me. His smile was candid, not so painful as in the past. I wanted to talk to him but the words wouldn't come. I waited for him to come close, to take my hands in his, to hold me in his arms. But he stayed there, still, as if he were seeking through his silence to make me understand something.

When I finally woke up I still felt complete and calm, as I had when I used to watch him sleeping after love.

*

For Antoine it wasn't just that Judith had left, it was also all the plans, all the dreams that they'd shared.

It might have been easier for him to tolerate their separation if he'd been able to tell himself that it was necessary, that there was nothing he could have done to avoid it. But he was gnawed by remorse and in his mind he kept reconstructing tirelessly their love affair, purging it of what had ruined it. He hadn't gone for a drink with his colleague that night; he hadn't gone up to her place; he'd left before it was too late. He was fed up with himself, he hated himself, he called himself all kinds of names—but he was angry with Judith too. She hadn't even given him a chance to explain himself. If he'd been able to at least speak to her, even for a moment, perhaps he could have talked her into staying. He would have made a thousand promises, showered her with words, with tender gestures, with surprises, and gradually they would have reclaimed their intimacy. Without saying a word she would have forgiven him and confidence would have been restored.

Against all hope, Antoine was still expecting Judith to come back. He was on the lookout for her at every street corner. He heard her climb the stairs, turn the key in the lock. When the phone rang he could make out her voice before he even answered. And every time she didn't appear, every time it was another voice on the phone, it was not his hope that weakened but reality itself. To his eyes the world disappeared, and he too became a dream—a dream that was no longer of any use.

And so, a few months later, when Antoine was offered a transfer to London, he accepted immediately.

*

Paris, 28 February 2001

A week since I've heard from Alain. I could call his office of course, there would be no risk, but for some time now I've been the one who revives our relationship. When we started to see each other, I would tell myself that since I didn't give Alain much of myself, I couldn't feel any pain. He was always the one who made the first move, and so I thought—wrongly, perhaps—that he needed me more than I needed him. I realize now that I miss him in spite of myself.

Paris, 4 March 2001

Terrible day at the bookstore. Every time the door opened I expected Alain to walk in. What's worse is that if he had come, I think I'd have pretended not to recognize him.

Paris, 5 March 2001

I don't love him; it's just that he occupies that space in my life now. The place was empty; he took it. I'm not even jealous. If Alain really were important to me, I would be constantly thinking about what he does with his wife, about the places they go to, the holidays they spend together.

True, I miss him, but simply because when he's there, I forget that I'm lonely.

Paris, 9 March 2001

This rather meaningless, rather mediocre relationship that's going nowhere exists in order to prove to me that I can't be in love any more, in order to show me what it's like to be with a man for whom one feels only desire—and contempt.

Paris, 11 March 2001

Still no word from Alain. This time I'll resist. I can be very determined sometimes, even when it hurts. And as time goes on, the harder it becomes to call him. It would be unnatural. We would both be uncomfortable, he because he would feel the need to explain, I because I would be the cause of his discomfort.

Paris, 12 March 2001

I sometimes wonder what Dad would have thought about all this, about my drifting. When I was in my teens he never thought twice about passing judgement on my friends. He thought they were either dull or dangerous. He never hesitated to tell me what he thought of them: "That one is so insipid! After you've met him ten times, on the eleventh time you can't remember who he is." Or, "That one will end up in prison, take my word—and so will you if you spend time with him." Later, when I joined him in New York, he was a little more subtle in his judgements. But as soon as I was with someone he couldn't stop himself from questioning me about "his intentions" and lamenting that he always saw me with men "who aren't good enough for you."

Now that he is no longer here I imagine him very differently. Death has changed him. He no longer reprimands me. I see him standing in front of me, looking helpless. He seems disarmed; he looks at me, smiles sadly, and I am sad to see him so despondent, so vulnerable. It's worse than his criticism.

Paris, 15 March 2001

Alain finally called me. The next day, he claimed, he was flying to Rome, to meet with a client. There was a kind of nonchalance in his voice, a little worry too, as if he were trying to find out if I was angry with him for not phoning me sooner. He asked if I was free the following week and promised to call on Saturday to make a date.

He won't call, I know he won't.

*

Antoine left Paris around the end of August 1992. At first London offered very little comfort. He'd stopped looking for Judith, but in this big city where he knew no one he could find nothing to mask the emptiness of his future. Later on he would have only very hazy memories of that time. He would remember his solitary evening walks in Covent Garden. He would think back to the mornings spent reading the papers on the terrace of a King's Road café. He would also recall the odours: the warm smell of beer drifting out of the pubs, the smell of the dead leaves that the wind swept around Sloane Square, the smell of the mist that wrapped the streets in the evening when he was on his way home from the office. But it would be hard for him to imagine his state of mind at that time because he had in a sense stopped feeling anything at all. He watched the continuous stream of people swarming in the tube and on the streets—all of them bustling, struggling, pushing and shoving, their determined looks, filled with certainties—and he didn't understand what drove them. Drained of all emotion, Antoine was incapable of recognizing it in others. It was as if he were living someone else's life, as if he were superfluous in this world.

*

Paris, 27 March 2001

I should have realized that matters would end that way. He was afraid I'd become attached to him or else he found someone else. Or maybe he was quite simply getting bored.

What's unbearable is the fact that I've been rejected. I should have seen it coming and dropped him myself. At least I'd have had the feeling that I hadn't given myself to him completely.

Then things would have been tidier. Still hoping that he'll call—that's truly pathetic.

Paris, 28 March 2001

This separation from Alain is as hard as it would have been had I really been in love. But if I'm in pain, doesn't it mean that I love him? No, not him, not a man like him. I can't have reached that point. All those dreams, all that stupid nostalgia—they're mine, totally mine.

He has nothing to do with it. It would have been the same with any other man. I cannot accept being lonely, that's all.

*

Gradually, Antoine got used to his new life. Now London did not feel as hostile as it had on his arrival. He'd started going out at night again. Determined not to become attached to anyone, he welcomed encounters without making them happen and let them end without holding on to them. Occasionally a relationship would last for several months, but in his memory it took up no more space than the ones that had lasted for just a few days. His life had taken on a monotonous and reassuring rhythm, punctuated only by two or three brief stays in Paris every year. These trips gave him a chance to see Séverine. They would have lunch together or, on fine days, go for a stroll in the Bois de Boulogne. Séverine now had a child whom she talked about a lot and Antoine, despite his lack of experience in the field, tried hard to ask intelligent questions about daycare, toys and sleep cycles.

Antoine had never enjoyed Séverine's company so much. He felt that he could tell her anything—even though he rarely had much to say—and knew that whatever advice or criticism she might offer, she would not judge him. The time when he'd thought he had different feelings for Séverine now seemed very remote. He watched her feed her baby, wipe his face, give him his pacifier, and he thought to himself that he was lucky, that they could very easily have fallen out of touch and nothing would have remained of the moments when they'd felt so close. In London, Antoine didn't often think of her, but she was a fixed point on his horizon, a benevolent voice that offered him the certainty of comfort. Antoine never mentioned Judith, and Séverine had every reason to think that he'd forgotten her. Antoine himself thought that he'd erased her from his memory. Deep in his work and concerned about being promoted, he no longer mused over the past. Sometimes a film or a piece of music would make a memory of Judith resurface briefly, but he never let himself stray too far along the road of memory.

If Antoine hadn't been so blind about his inner life, he might have realized that the place Judith had occupied there was still intact. Directing his attention elsewhere, he had allowed his recollections of Judith to grow in his memory. Like an invisible excrescence, that memory had been transformed and, indifferent to the silence of his heart, had itself been wrapped in silence. Crouching in the depths of his being, feeding only on bits of the past that were buried very deep in his consciousness, the memory waited for its hour to come, certain that it couldn't die, confident that it would reappear some day to set his existence ablaze once again.

3

Quotidien de Nice,
Wednesday 28 August 2002

SUSPICIOUS DEATH OF JOURNALIST VIRGINIE RIVIÈRE

The body of Virginie Rivière was discovered on a beach in Nice yesterday afternoon. Police assume the death was caused by drowning, but scratches on the young woman's arms and shoulders raise the possibility that she was the victim of an attack. "At this point the possibility of homicide cannot be excluded," declared a police spokesperson at a press conference.

According to a sister of Ms. Rivière, who identified the body, the young journalist swam every morning before going to work. "She was an excellent swimmer. Of course accidents can happen. In her case, though, it's hard to imagine," she says.

A correspondent with the *Quotidien de Nice* since September 2000, Rivière published a number of pieces on drug trafficking on the Côte d'Azur. According to her sister she had received several anonymous letters, but was determined not to give in to intimidation.

The reaction of her colleagues was dismay. "We're shocked. Virginie was a wonderful colleague, kind, always smiling, always ready to help others. She was irreplaceable," declared editor-in-chief Roland Auger.

*

Paris, 15 May 2001

Too many changes in my life and once again I don't really know how to pick up the thread. I'd never have thought it could happen.

I no longer fear that we'll separate. I have just one concern: to lose nothing of this moment.

Paris, 19 May 2001

I said that I'd never have thought it could happen: that's not quite true. When I moved to New York nine years ago I had vague hopes of a letter from Antoine.

In my anger I'd left him without a forwarding address, without telling him where I was going. I felt betrayed. I hated him and I hated myself for still being in love with him. And yet I told myself that if he'd really wanted, he could have found me. And since I've come back to Paris, I have to admit that I would sometimes think I recognized him on the street. I would tell myself, "There's a chance that he still lives in Montmartre, maybe he still goes to that café..."

When he walked into the bookstore the other day, I felt so helpless, so disoriented. I didn't want him to see me. If we'd been anywhere else, in a store or on the street, I think I would have fled. I'd dreamed so much of that moment, imagined it in so many forms, it no longer seemed possible that one day it would happen. It was as if by thinking about it too much, I'd exhausted the reality of it.

He didn't see me right away. He was strolling between the shelves; he didn't seem too sure of what he was looking for. From the corner of my eye I watched him choose some books almost at random, leaf through them, then put them back on the shelf. I stood there, motionless. I didn't want to attract his attention. I was so excited, so anxious, that I didn't even try to anticipate what I'd say to him. When he finally came up to the cash register, I put my head down, pretending to be absorbed in my accounts. But before I even looked up, I heard him say my name. It was not even a question; his voice held neither surprise nor hesitation. He simply looked relieved, as if he'd always known that this moment would arrive.

*

That was in May. More than nine years since Judith had disappeared from Antoine's life.

He was in Paris to meet some clients and he'd had lunch with Séverine. Before getting back on the train to London he'd gone walking around the Quartier Latin.

Now that he was working he didn't often get a chance to stroll around, and those few hours spent going from one bookstore to another ranked among his most prized pleasures. Often he would first make his way towards the bookstalls along the Seine, but this time, he'd decided to leave his usual route and venture to the other side of boulevard Saint-Germain.

It had started to rain and Antoine had taken shelter in a small art bookstore near the Panthéon. He paged through a few books absentmindedly while he waited for the rain to stop. Seeing a book on Monet's *Les Nymphéas*, he thought about Séverine—Monet was her favourite painter—and since it would soon be her birthday, he decided to buy it for her.

It was as he was approaching the counter with the large book under his arm that he recognized her. Her head was bent over a ledger sheet and she seemed to be concentrating hard, absent from the world around her. Her black hair covered half her face, offering only a glimpse of her pale, delicate mouth and the pointed chin that gave her an impish look. For a moment Antoine was disconcerted. It was as if something in him were resisting, as if faced with surprise, faced with the certainty that it was her, he had felt like hesitating a little longer.

He had the feeling that this moment was etched inside him, that it had always existed. Everything was back to normal, now he just had to let himself go; tremendous self-confidence, like a gentle warmth, spread through him. He walked up and placed the book on the counter. Before she even raised her head he could feel her eyes on him. And when she finally looked at him, it was as if she was answering him, as if she had guessed his surprise.

They spent the evening together, and after dinner in a restaurant they went to Judith's place. Later, when Antoine tried to piece together that first night, he wouldn't be able to recall the details. He would see himself lying beside her, his hand on her damp belly, and he would simply remember that to every kiss he placed on her body, Judith responded with a murmur, a faint lament, a "yes" that became a "no." But all the rest would stay drowned in his imagination. He wouldn't be able to recall the words she'd whispered in his ear, or what he'd said in reply. Only minor details came back to him: her dark red nail polish, the cool air that came in the badly closed window, the smell of alcohol from the half-empty wine glass on the bedside table.

He would try in vain to remember Judith's caresses, recall what she had liked. He couldn't even be sure he'd come that night. And for a long time he would search his memory to see whether in Judith's look, in one of her smiles, there was some sign that could have warned him of what would come next, of the abyss they'd fallen into.

*

Paris, 24 May 2001

Now that he is here, I realize how empty my life has been without him. My time in New York after leaving him now seems to be merely an interlude, a sustained interruption that should never have happened. I try to remember how I used to fill my time. I try to picture myself at the gallery, in my apartment, strolling around SoHo, and what I see is an unchanging and quiet life, strange, with no worries and no attachments. And those years seem all the more vain to me, all the more hollow, all the more empty because I didn't even hope to find Antoine again. I wonder now how I could have wanted to go on without that hope. In any case, no matter what happens I'll never go back to that life. If I were to lose him again it really would be the end.

*

Shortly after he went back to London, Antoine had phoned Nathalie to tell her that it was over. She'd practically burst out laughing. "Sure, Antoine, and a week from now you'll call me back and everything will start again like before. You think I don't know you? But I understand. You want to believe you're still free. You want to believe that you can get along without me."

He imagined her sitting on her bed, holding a cigarette. While she was talking to him she might already be flipping through her address book in search of the man who would keep her company tonight. This time, though, Antoine didn't feel the slightest twinge of jealousy. He didn't try to contradict her, scoff at her, wound her. He wondered how he could have been—or at least thought he was—so in love with her, how he'd been able to accept all those lies, those humiliations, and every time come back to her as if he was the one who'd hurt her.

Ever since he'd gotten back together with Judith, Nathalie had become a stranger to him. And as much as his past feelings now seemed incomprehensible, so did he now understand her: her fragility, her frantic desire to exist for others, the inadequacy of her dreams. He was free of her; he could afford to be generous. He would have been almost ready to recognize her qualities—she had a lovely laugh, told stories well, was a good cook—if he'd been sure that she was well and truly out of his life and that she wouldn't somehow try to force her way back in.

*

Paris, 28 May 2001

Back to Paris. I spent the weekend in London with Antoine and my heart is heavy because I'm alone again.

Every time we separate I sense some concern on his part, as if he is afraid I'll disappear again. In the restaurant on Saturday he kept asking me about my childhood, my father, my education. He was curious to know where I'd lived, who my friends were, where I went on holiday. I don't doubt his sincerity; he wants to make up for lost time. But I can't help thinking that he also wants to gather as much information as he can about me in case I should disappear. I'd have liked to reassure him, to tell him that I'd never go away again, that nothing could come between us now no matter what, but it didn't seem very natural. I don't want to have to prove to him that I love him; for me, it's obvious—and when we try too hard to prove something obvious, doesn't it mean fundamentally that we have some doubts?

*

The women he had known, the ones he'd wished would love him, now seemed to him lifeless, flavourless. He wondered how he could have found them so appealing. He tried to recall their faces and realized now how insipid they were, frozen in the anticipation of pleasure. Judith's face, in contrast, was always changing, did not let itself be defined by the way people looked at her. Antoine observed her, sitting on the floor, her back against the sofa, deep in a detective novel. Her face, calm, seemed constantly about to be transformed into a new expression as if, inaccessible to desire, it produced, at every moment, the reality of its presence. Even motionless it contained a sea of movement, like the film of a plant played on fast-forward, in which every frame reveals a minuscule change. Antoine had no desire to kiss her or touch her, he allowed himself to gaze at her as if hypnotized. He had the feeling that this face contained his entire future.

*

When Séverine saw Antoine approaching, she noticed neither his rather threadbare suit nor the yellowed collar of his shirt nor the shadows under his eyes. All she saw was his smile—and it had never seemed so candid, so warm, so free. Antoine appeared taller than usual to her, his movements more sweeping, his appearance more jaunty. She noticed that, for the first time, he was using his hands when he spoke.

"What's happened to you? You're radiant..."
"Yes... I mean..."
He looked at her, smiling, not sure how to begin.
"It's incredible... I... I saw Judith..."
He broke off, as if he himself were trying to take the measure of what had happened to him. Séverine stared at him, stunned.

"It was the last time I came to Paris. It was raining so I ducked into a bookstore and . . . she was there . . . Seeing her again like that after nearly ten years . . . it was . . . I don't think I've ever been so happy . . ."

Séverine didn't know what to say. Her head was buzzing with questions. She remembered Antoine's distress when Judith had left him. She'd never understood why, if they loved one another so much, Judith hadn't even given him a chance to explain himself before she left. But Antoine seemed so peaceful now, so confident in the future that she hadn't wanted to disturb his joy with her questions. She merely smiled at him, at once tender and concerned, telling herself that a happiness that seems so complete was probably not meant to last.

*

Paris, 11 June 2001

Tedious day at the bookstore. I spent my time thinking about Antoine. I miss him—and I don't know if it's because we were so good together last Saturday or because I'm afraid that moment will never return.

We woke up later than usual that morning. We were very hungry so we went out right away and had breakfast in a café on King's Road, a few minutes from his place. That afternoon we drove to Hampstead Heath and took a long walk.

Deep inside the wood, we ran into other couples who sometimes smiled at us. Their obvious happiness reassured us and made us happy. We talked about ourselves, about our childhoods, our parents. I realized that in fact I didn't know much about Antoine, and I listened intently as he talked about his dreams and his setbacks and disappointments in love, his teenage bad behaviour and his extravagances. I felt at the same time very close to him yet oddly detached—a little as if we'd just met, as if we were still in the early stages of love and not yet sure if it would work out.

It started to rain, but instead of taking shelter in a café like other people, we chose to go on walking in the woods. Despite the fine drizzle we could still catch glimpses of the sun. A moment later, out of the blue, we started to sing—songs from childhood, suddenly remembered, that we were thrilled to realize we both knew. I felt that those songs created a special bond between us and lent a kind of depth to our relationship. And for the first time since we'd met up again I felt the same pleasure, the same lightness at being with him as I had nine years earlier, in Paris. Very briefly I thought about nothing but him, but us—nothing else existed for me. I had stopped worrying about the future, because I felt that the future didn't matter anymore.

We made our way back to the car. We were soaking wet and anxious to get inside and dry ourselves. Once we were back at his place we fixed a big bowl of salad and spent the evening watching an old American movie on TV. I no longer felt the way I'd felt a while before and I was already reminding myself that the next day I would have to go back to Paris. But I was certain now that what we'd felt for one another years ago was intact and that we still had access to the path that led to it.

*

When Judith emerged from the shower, Antoine was on the phone. Leaning against the wall in the vestibule, head down, he hardly noticed her. He was speaking very softly, muttering. Judith went to the kitchen to make tea. From there, she could hear bits of conversation: "Listen, I thought we'd turned the page . . . I don't understand, we made no promises . . . Think whatever you want, for me it really is over . . ."

A few moments later Antoine went back to the bedroom. Judith was sitting on the bed, holding a cup of tea. She seemed to be absorbed in her book and didn't even look up when he came in. Antoine stood for a few moments facing the bed. He knew that he owed Judith an explanation, but he would have preferred her to make the first move. It would have been easier then for him to put on a detached tone of voice and convince her that she had no reason to doubt him. In contrast, by being the one to break the silence he would necessarily appear to be giving the conversation more importance than he would have wanted.

"That was Nathalie," he said, getting into his pyjamas.

"Ah," said Judith, without taking her nose out of her book.

"I explained to her that it was over."

"I thought she already knew."

"She does, but she won't take it seriously. Not that she particularly wants me, but she isn't used to being told no."

Judith did not doubt Antoine's sincerity, but she couldn't help thinking that only a few weeks ago he was still with Nathalie, calling her every evening, spending his nights with her.

"Has she ever been here?"

"Yes, I mean . . . not very often. I went to her place."

Judith bristled. Antoine knew perfectly well what she was thinking about. He didn't know what to say. All his denials would only reinforce Judith's suspicions, whet her curiosity.

"And . . . what was she like?"

Antoine pretended that he didn't understand.

"I don't know . . . around thirty, average height, blond, green eyes . . ."

"You know very well that's not what I mean."

Judith was determined to see it through to the end. She was angry with herself for going so far, probably she never should have started, but it was too late now. She wanted to know everything. Even if there was something a little demeaning about asking such questions, even if she knew that it would be painful, that it would lead nowhere, that they would fall asleep each on their own side of the bed, irritated, furious, bitter, and that the next morning it would take a long time to break the silence.

"Look, Judith . . ."

"It's all right, I'm not jealous, just curious."

She did her best to smile, to make him believe that she really was indifferent. But in her expression there was a toughness that Antoine had never seen before. He sighed and finally told her, exasperated, "She was selfish. About everything. In her pleasure and in everything else."

"But isn't that what you loved, basically?"

Judith was giving him a mischievous, nearly malicious look.

"Maybe. But it didn't make me happy."

*

"It's funny, I can't smell you."

"What do you mean?"

"You don't smell of anything . . . your skin has no smell at all."

"Maybe. I've never thought about it. People don't smell their own odour."

Lying beside Judith, Antoine took his hand away from hers. He was silent.

"Does it bother you that I don't smell of anything?"

"No, not at all. It's just that all the women I . . . I mean, it's just that it's a little unusual."

Antoine began to turn red. Not much, just enough to be aware of it himself. Judith wouldn't have minded if he had been more open. If he had simply said, "All the women I've known smelled of something. One smelled of, let's say, vanilla, another of freshly mown grass, another of sandalwood. You, though, smell of nothing. But it doesn't matter, I love you the way you are." And that would have been that. Judith wouldn't have started to think about all those women who supposedly smelled so good. What she couldn't stand was that he didn't even want to talk about it. He wanted to make her think that all those years hadn't mattered, as if he had never doubted that they'd get together again some day.

*

Judith got up to make coffee. The sun bathed the kitchen in an amber, dense, nearly palpable light. It was the first time they'd made love in the afternoon.

Antoine approached her. He wasn't sure if she'd heard him. Gently, he laid his hand on her shoulder. She didn't turn around. Bending over the counter she was measuring ground coffee into the filter, a spoonful at a time, her movements slow and precise. Antoine wrapped Judith in his arms, deftly slipped his hands under her dressing gown. One wandered across her stomach for a while, then settled on her breasts, while the other wedged itself between her legs. When he felt Judith's body stiffen, Antoine loosened his hold. He lifted her hair and deposited a kiss in the hollow on the back of her neck, as if to apologize for his impudence.

Judith left the kitchen and when she came back, she found Antoine sitting at the small table, leafing through the paper from the day before. She poured coffee and sat across from him.

"And who was it before Nathalie?"

The question caught Antoine unawares. He tried to mask his surprise by pretending to be absorbed in his newspaper, but from the nervous way he moved, Judith could tell that he didn't know how to reply.

"What do you mean, before Nathalie?"

Impassively, like a teacher patiently repeating the same explanation to a slightly dim pupil, she said again, "I mean, who were you with before Nathalie?"

"I don't know, I was on my own for a while and . . . but what difference does it make?"

"Nothing, I'm just curious, that's all."

"All right, I was . . . there were a few affairs that didn't work out and . . ."

"But serious affairs. Nathalie wasn't the only one, was she?"

"No, there was one other, but it didn't really count . . ."

"How long were you together?"

"I can't remember, maybe three or four years."

"Four years! That's a long time for a relationship that didn't matter. And . . . what was her name?"

"Virginie."

Judith said nothing. She could see that Antoine wouldn't say a thing unless she wormed it out of him. So that he wouldn't feel she was subjecting him to an interrogation, she picked up a section of the newspaper and started to read. A few minutes later she got up, poured herself more coffee, then pretended to plunge back into her reading. With her face half-hidden by the newspaper she went on. "How did you meet?"

"She was a journalist. She'd come to interview me about European monetary policy. Then a few days later she called me again, we got together and that's it."

"So she's the one who chased after you?"

"You could say that, yes."

"What was she like physically?"

Antoine looked at her silently again, disconcerted. He sensed that nothing would calm her. He had to let her finish, let her exhaust herself. By evening she would be loving again, she'd be mad at herself and since she could never bring herself to apologize, she would say simply, "I don't know what's going on with me, I don't know why I'm like that. I'm happy with you, but I can't help myself. I'm jealous, terribly jealous." In an attempt to put an end to this conversation that was leading nowhere, he said, "Why are you being so hard on yourself, Judith? We're together, isn't that what matters?"

"No, you don't understand. What I want is to love you the way I did before. But we've changed too much. I know very well that all those relationships don't mean a thing, but they still changed us. When you live with someone that person leaves a mark. And you have marks all over you."

*

Paris, 21 June 2001

I can't stop thinking about Antoine, about the first Antoine, the one I knew nine years ago. I remember now that the ambiguity of his body on mine elated me and at the same time moved me. His caresses were so gentle, as I wanted mine to be—so much so that I practically felt as if I was loving a reflection of myself: his hands, brushing my skin, seemed to obey my own will and it seemed to me that his mouth was kissing me as I would have kissed myself if I'd been Antoine.

I existed because he loved me and I loved him because he made me exist. Banished from my own body, from my thoughts, my habits, it was myself whom I found, plunged into him because his desire had traced my presence in the innermost recesses of his life. And when I left it was not only him that I lost, it was myself, the self I had become in him.

*

"That girl you knew back then, the lawyer, do you still see her?"

Antoine turned towards Judith, surprised. They had spent the day walking around London, first in Hyde Park, then in Kensington and finally on the banks of the Thames. They'd come home exhausted. After wolfing down a pizza in front of the TV, Antoine had washed and put on pyjamas, impatient to get into bed. He was reading, stretched out, glancing now and then at Judith, watching her get undressed, brush her teeth, wash her face. Too tired to make love, he just wanted to hold her in his arms for a moment, then go to sleep. But he sensed that Judith wouldn't let go easily. He responded in a tone that he hoped was neutral, but that already betrayed his impatience.

"Séverine? Yes, now and then."

"What's become of her?"

"She's still a lawyer."

"Married?"

"Yes."

"Do you know her husband?"

"Not really. I've met him a couple of times..."

"So you see one another alone?"

"Yes."

"And what do you do when you're together?"

"Nothing, we have lunch in a restaurant. Sometimes we walk for a while."

"You've never gone further?"

"No."

"Really?"

"Yes, really."

"I find that hard to believe."

"I know."

"It's not that I doubt you, Antoine. But a relationship that lasts like that . . . and you've never wanted to go further?"

"Maybe at the beginning. But that was before you and I met."

"What about her?"

"I don't know. I don't think so."

"Maybe she's always loved you and was just waiting for you to make a move . . ."

"No, I'd be surprised . . ."

"And if she weren't married, if you weren't with me . . . ?"

"That's hypothetical. Maybe . . . but I also think that we could simply be friends."

Judith shot him a look that was half-harsh, half-tender, like a mother whose child has just told a whopper.

"Do you really think you'd still be friends if there hadn't been an attraction on one side or the other?" And without giving him time to reply, she went on. "I'm not convinced. You want to think that friendship is possible because you don't want to admit that physical attraction counts for so much in our choices. But in fact men and women have no reason to be friends."

Antoine wasn't in the mood to reply. After a long silence he switched off the light. Motionless, he listened to Judith's breathing get deeper and deeper. In the darkness, he tried to make out her profile, the curve of her forehead, the slight arch of her nose. He could have tried to comfort her, but he no longer had the courage. He knew that the next day the tension between them would build again.

*

London, 5 July 2001

For a week now I've been living at Antoine's place. I handed in my resignation to the bookstore. Most of my things I left in Paris, bringing only some clothes and a few books. It was Antoine who insisted that I move in. He was tired of being separated during the week, he wanted us to live like a "real couple." He may be right. It will be good for us to be together every day. The constant separations, the excitement of getting together again on Friday, the melancholy of Sunday night—it's not natural. He doesn't say so, but I'm sure he thinks that if we live together I won't be so jealous. After all, I'll see him every morning, every night, sometimes even at lunchtime. I'll no longer have reason to doubt him. What he doesn't understand is that I trust him, that I know he won't cheat on me. What I'm jealous of is his past.

*

London, 7 July 2001

I don't know why I behave like that. I act as if I'm dead set on destroying what's most precious to me. I think about Dad. I imagine him looking sadly at me. "You've got everything you need to be happy, Judith. You finally have what you want: a man you love, who loves you, a comfortable life with no worries. You can get married now, have children. What more do you want?" I know he's right. And yet I can't stop myself from saying to him in my head, "You don't understand. It's not about your happiness, it's about mine. And I don't want a quiet life, safe and flat..."

Maybe I'm actually trying to make myself jealous. Otherwise it would be too easy. I need obstacles if I'm to go on loving. Maybe, too, I don't love him as much as I'd like to. Thinking about the others, about the women who shared his life for a while, is a way to make him more desirable to me. Others have loved him so I'm right to hold on to him. And everything they've had is still there for me to win over . . .

Antoine is right; I'm only hurting myself. Everything is mixed up in my head. Really, I'm lucky to have him. I'm lucky that he puts up with me, in spite of all my obsessions and my fears.

*

"Do you fancy her?"

"I beg you, Judith, stop."

"You didn't see yourself! Your eyes were glued to her as if . . ."

"Oh, all right, I looked at her. So what?"

They had arranged to meet at a small Greek restaurant in Bloomsbury. Antoine said nothing. For several nights he hadn't been sleeping well and he seemed very preoccupied by work. The waitress, a plump young woman with an insipid face and an ample bosom, had come up to them, smiling, and taken their order patiently, describing the dishes in detail. Antoine, encouraged perhaps by the young woman's generous smile, couldn't help focusing on her bosom. And without thinking too much about Judith, he'd followed the waitress with his eyes—her swaying walk, her chubby legs, her heavy, sweet perfume—until she disappeared behind the bar.

Judith did her best to suppress her anger. She lit a cigarette, pushed back her chair, crossed and uncrossed her legs several times and then in a dry tone that she hoped was indifferent: "I said it for you, that's all. You look a little ridiculous and that makes me sad."

Antoine didn't reply. A few weeks earlier he would probably have taken her hands, moved closer to her, looked her in the eyes. He might have stroked her hair as well, pulled it back behind her ears to have a better look at her face, and eventually Judith would have smiled at him. Then she would have told him about her day, the film she wanted to see, as if nothing had happened. But Antoine didn't feel like making any efforts. He was tired of reassuring her, of calming her anxiety, of soothing her jealousy. He was jealous too. He waited till the waitress had brought their appetizers before breaking the silence.

"That guy you were talking about the other day, Laurent something or other, do you still see him?"

Judith seemed surprised.

"No."

"What is it he does? Something in the arts, right?"

"Cultural attaché at the consulate."

"Where did you meet?"

"At my father's gallery."

"What happened? Was he the one who chased after you?"

"In a way, yes."

"And you didn't put up much resistance..."

"No. I'd just left David and I didn't really want to be alone..."

"So you threw yourself into the arms of the first man who showed up."

"Not really. Laurent had his flaws, but he was terribly charming and he knew a lot of things. He made me laugh. And then..."

"And then?"

"And then nothing. We had some good times together but it's been over for a long time. I don't think about him any more, it's you who made me talk about him."

Judith seemed so calm, so reasonable when she talked about her own love life. Antoine sensed that she was telling him just enough to rouse his curiosity. She could have reassured him easily if she'd wanted.

She could have suppressed all his doubts by saying, "I spent two years with Laurent, but I wasn't in love with him. None of that matters to me, it never did. Let's stop talking about him. Today I only think about you, I don't imagine myself with anyone else." But Judith deliberately let him go on.

"You were in love with him though, weren't you?"

"In love—not really. I just liked him, that's all."

"What was it you liked about him?"

"I don't know, I liked him, I enjoyed being with him."

"Did you live together?"

"No, but towards the end I was spending a lot of time at his place."

"You never thought about moving in with him, about getting married?"

"He did maybe, but I didn't. In any case we never talked about it. I left before that."

"Why?"

"He was suffocating me. He had all kinds of weird habits. In the beginning I thought he was entertaining, but at the end he bored me. He wanted his obsessions to be taken seriously. He became more and more demanding..."

"What kind of obsessions?"

"I don't know, he was . . . He liked everything neat and tidy. I couldn't leave a cup of tea lying around without his reprimanding me. I couldn't touch his books because apparently I was liable to damage the binding . . . And he had strong ideas about everything, about how to set the table, about the films that had to be seen and how to talk about them. He showered me with presents, clothes mainly, but that was because he didn't like the way I dressed. He thought I didn't care enough about my appearance. The worst thing is, he was sure he was making me happy. He loved himself so completely he couldn't imagine that someone might not feel privileged to be loved by him. And it was the same for everything, the *mise en scène* continued even . . ."

"Even?"

Judith was silent, staring at her plate, which she hadn't touched. All sorts of images were coming back to her, jostling together in her head. All the things that Laurent made her do, his morbid sensuality, his meticulous search for pleasure for pleasure's sake—now it all disgusted her. She wondered how she could have agreed to those ridiculous games without the slightest resistance, without feeling even the smallest particle of shame or anger. She saw herself lying on the bed, naked, blindfolded. In the flickering candlelight he liked to bite her, scratch her, pour hot wax over her body. Judith went along with everything, as if his demands, even the strangest ones, were perfectly normal. But she was more angry with herself than with Laurent. She was angry not simply for having gone along obediently with all of those games, but for having so readily let Laurent's desires displace her own. Facing Antoine, who was looking at her, at once worried and tender, she felt naked, vulnerable, as if he had guessed what she was remembering, as if his jealousy had given him the power to see into her.

That night Antoine fell asleep before Judith, who couldn't sleep a wink, restless because of her memories. She turned to him and put her arm around his waist. Almost immediately his whole body shivered, as if his skin had suddenly been covered with light. With the tips of her fingers she stroked his hairy chest, let her hand run down his hips, stopped between his legs. Slowly, Antoine turned to her, eyes half-closed as if he were doing some routine task, and started to touch her, to kiss her breasts. Antoine's nonchalance, his apparent indifference, gave her more pleasure than his words of love and his customary intense looks. Judith felt at once light and empty, exquisitely empty, as if she no longer had to carry the weight of Antoine's desire. And that night she came with him as she never had before, as if she didn't know him, as if she had never loved him.

*

London, 15 *July* 2001

Last night I made a serious effort. During the day I tidied the apartment, did the grocery shopping, bought flowers. Then I prepared as best I could a "real meal": main course, salad, cheese, dessert. When Antoine arrived the table was set—I'd even ironed the cloth and the napkins. He was very surprised, very touched as well, and he kissed me more tenderly than usual. He knew that it was my way of apologizing for being so difficult these past days, but still he asked, "What are we celebrating?" I didn't want to reply. It's been two months since we ran into each other at the bookstore. But I didn't want to talk about us, especially not about the past and everything that was tormenting me.

Antoine was more relaxed than usual, even garrulous, talking about his work, his colleagues. He described to me the head of the Paris office—a gruff man with an enormous belly and a thin voice who was always giving him a hard time. He imitated him and it made me laugh. I felt very close to him.

Afterwards, we made love. In the dark my desire was strong, but I was too tired to come so I pretended. I don't know if he realized it but before he fell asleep he put his arm around my waist and whispered in my ear. "You know, for me nothing has changed . . . and nothing will change."

*

While he was getting dressed, Antoine looked at Judith as she slept. She appeared so tender, so affectionate in her sleep. He felt that she took the shape of all his thoughts of gentleness and peace, like a wax model of a dream. At that moment it seemed to him that if he stroked her face, if he lifted the long black lock of hair that fell like a question mark onto her right cheek, she would half-open her eyes, smile at him and hold out her arms for a cuddle, and then he would join her.

As if she had felt his eyes on her, she turned around. Antoine noticed that she was wearing his shirt, the one he'd put on at the office the day before. He was touched, and also reassured. Since she had moved in with him, Judith had silently taken possession of the premises, rearranging the furniture, redecorating the bedrooms. Now she was even appropriating his clothes. Antoine saw it as a sign of trust, an assurance that she wouldn't go away again, despite her bitterness and her jealousy.

Antoine tried to remember what Judith had looked like when he met her nine years earlier. But he could only recall scattered details: long afternoons spent together, reading and eating bread and Nutella, walks in the Bois de Boulogne and the Jardin du Luxembourg, their interminable telephone conversations on nights when they weren't sleeping together. One memory in particular had stuck with him nearly intact, and had recently come back, more intense than ever. One Saturday morning he and Judith both woke earlier than usual. It must have been five o'clock or half-past, and sunlight was already streaming into the bedroom. They threw on some clothes and went out. Antoine had to be at a friend's place at eight o'clock to wait for some delivery or other and as the métro was on strike, they'd decided to walk. It was a long way; Antoine lived near Montmartre at the time and his friend's place was on the avenue de Versailles, a few minutes from the Bois de Boulogne.

They had walked hand in hand through the deserted streets. The sun, already warm, made the morning mist nearly palpable. The air was still heavy with the smells of the night. Antoine remembered the sound of their footsteps that rang out on the damp pavement and seemed to urge them to remain silent. Several times he'd been about to say something, but at the last moment he decided against it.

He had mentally gone over this walk through the silent city so many times, hoping to find some detail of Judith's face, a smile he wouldn't have noticed but that was still inscribed in his memory. That moment contained such an elusive aura, such a warm and pure stillness that he sometimes wondered if he'd only dreamed it. Perhaps because of the separation that had followed, the moment had become for Antoine the very emblem of what their life together could have been.

As he was knotting his tie, Antoine continued to gaze at Judith asleep. That was the image he wanted to take along with him to the office. He knew that when he came home that evening they would probably have another painful talk. She would question him again about God knows whom and he would let himself be carried along. She would tell him about some other man she'd known, whom she'd lived with, and then he would start interrogating her. Dropping all sense of propriety, all dignity, he would demand details. He would imagine her happiness, her pleasure with the other man, as if he himself no longer existed, as if there was no one but Judith and her past. And as on other evenings, the same pitiful thoughts would accompany him, alone, in his sleep.

How had they got to this point? It was as if both of them, alarmed at having achieved their goal, now wanted to wreck their happiness so they could go on looking for it. Yet in spite of all the bitterness, all the jealousy, Antoine had no doubt that everything would eventually go back to normal. He recalled their silent walk nine years earlier, he saw himself walking with Judith, their joy barely visible on their serene faces, and he knew that the crisis would pass, that they would find a way to love one another again.

But when he recalled that walk, Antoine never went beyond it. He didn't ask himself how the day had ended and maybe wasn't even aware that only a few weeks after that fantastic moment he had cheated on Judith with Kate Waterton.

*

London, 28 *July* 2001

The other night the light from the streetlamps came into the bedroom through the partly open window. We weren't used to making love in the light. It was as if a white strip that slashed the darkness had lodged on

Antoine's face. I was on top. Watching him. I couldn't really see the expression on his face. Neither desire nor pleasure nor boredom nor anxiety. He appeared to be rather serene—but not like someone who has everything he wants, rather like someone who has nothing more to hope for.

London, 4 August 2001

I didn't think I was capable of feeling such jealousy. It arrived all at once. Antoine, the vast memory of our first meeting, my disappointment, my frustration at not finding my feelings as I'd left them... I had to find a reason, find those responsible. He hadn't spent those nine years thinking about me, that was obvious. He'd known other women; he'd known happy days, disappointments, hopes that he would never share. He'd left something of himself behind in each of those relationships. Those women had seen him happy, anxious, enthusiastic, melancholy. They'd taken away with them thousands of moments, of secrets, and confessions that he wasn't even aware of. Subtly, unbeknownst to him, they continued to alter the course of his life. They'd erected a wall of memories between us.

London, 5 August 2001

My jealousy is like a grim, dingy Rome where, inexorably, all roads of my consciousness lead.

*

Antoine had said nothing to Judith. He feared her reaction and didn't feel like having to explain himself again. If he had to see Séverine in secret, so be it. He was not about to cut all ties with her just so Judith's jealously wouldn't suffer. Her jealousy was all the more paradoxical because Antoine had never desired Séverine less than now. Now that he and Judith were together, he couldn't see Séverine as anything but a friend and he was free to confide in her with no ulterior motive. That morning as he was walking to the bistro near the Madeleine where they were in the habit of going for lunch, Antoine felt more than ever the need to open his heart to his friend. He would have liked to tell her about Judith's suspicions and jealousy, the everlasting interrogations, the constant impression that he was being watched. It seemed to him that Séverine, as an objective witness, could have helped him understand how they'd got to that point. Talking to her, he'd have been able to describe his own feelings.

He could have told Séverine what Judith no longer wanted to hear, that her gaze, darkened by suspicion, bitterness and fear, even kept her from understanding; that he loved her, that nothing else mattered for him, but that his certainty had gradually become a pain from which he could be neither healed nor extricated. In the imaginary exchanges he drew up, Séverine tried hard to give him advice, to reassure him. She was convinced that everything would be sorted out, that it was just a passing crisis. She encouraged him to be patient, to listen to Judith, comfort her, ignore her provocations.

But when Antoine arrived at the café and saw the radiant Séverine holding her new baby, he realized it would be unfair to lay out his worries and his sorrow. Rather than disturb her joy he did his best to share it, listening as intently as he could to what she had to say about nannies, diapers and colic. Antoine learned that the oldest child now went to school and that his little brother, to whom Séverine was giving a bottle, was starting to teethe. Learning about these small details of everyday life was good for him. They took him away from himself a little. He told himself that if he listened to Séverine long enough, part of her smooth, peaceful existence would somehow seep into his own.

After so many tormented days he now took more solace from contemplating the fullness of another's life than from dissecting his own, which always revealed new pains.

*

London, 14 August 2001

Antoine is working very hard these days. He leaves especially early, before I'm awake, and he's never home before eight. He's in no hurry to come home and I can't really blame him. For some time now we've been speaking less and less, to avoid one of those endless discussions about relationships in the past.

The last time it was truly painful. Antoine started it. I had my period, I felt exhausted and all I wanted to do was read for a while and then go to sleep. Antoine, though, wanted to talk. Rather, he wanted to make me talk, encouraged me to tell him about my life before him. He assumed a detached tone of voice, as if it were just playful curiosity, a matter of exchanging some banal words before going to sleep. But in fact, all those questions had just one goal: to find out more about the others, especially Alain. I didn't feel like reassuring him, so I said as little as possible. I let him suppose what he wanted. He knew that it had been hard for me to break up with Alain. He had deduced that I'd loved him and I didn't try to contradict him. I allowed him to doubt, imagine, dream about what happiness could have been like for me without him. Since I said nothing about Alain, it meant that he must have filled a tremendous place in my life. For Antoine, my silence had opened an abyss of love.

London, 17 August 2001

I should stop asking myself so many questions and live a little more, one day at a time. But basically I know why I insist so much on preventing myself from being happy: because I'm afraid of not being happy, of no longer being happy with Antoine. What I fear most is that our relationship will languish, that it will end up like all the others, that I'll be bored with everyday life. I've waited too long, dreamed too much to accept that.

*

Antoine was lying on the bed, watching Judith take her shower. The bathroom light was off and through the partly open door he could see only her silhouette. Facing the shower, head cocked to one side, Judith was letting the water run over her nearly motionless body. Her long black hair covered her face. After a moment, Antoine got up. He went into the bathroom. "Are you all right?" Judith didn't answer. Antoine took off his briefs and got into the tub. He placed his hand on her shoulder. Her skin was warm under the scalding shower. Antoine put his other hand on Judith's hip, stroked her belly, then moved up to her breasts. Judith did not react. He pressed himself against her, put his fingers on her pubis, as if to hide it, as if to protect her modesty. Still she didn't move. He entered her slowly. He felt her barely quiver. Not a sound came from her mouth; only her breathing seemed to speed up a little. Automatically, as if from habit, he touched her clitoris, and her legs seemed to him to part slightly. He felt her come, a few spasms that took him a little deeper inside her. Judith was still silent, as if she had let her body, guided by its will alone, act without her. Antoine withdrew. Standing behind Judith, arms dangling, he hesitated briefly. He would have liked to kiss her, force her to turn towards him, take her face in his hands. But he was afraid that she'd start crying. Or had she already started? He imagined her tears, imperceptible among the drops of water that ran down her body. He wouldn't have known how to comfort her. Finally, he went back to the bed, lay down, his body still wet, and fell asleep without knowing if she'd come back to join him.

*

London, 20 August 2001

Why do I torment myself like this? I know that he loves me, that I have no reason to doubt him. I ought to be so happy to have been reunited with him. But I realize I'm still angry. I'm angry with him for ruining everything the first time, I'm angry with him for not being equal to my memory of him—all that is ridiculous and unfair but I can't do anything about it.

London, 21 August 2001

It's not just that I want to make Antoine jealous, it's also because more and more I can't stand the thought that I myself have known other men. It seems to me that because of that I can't be with him entirely. I realize now that they mattered far more than I thought at the time. David and Laurent I allowed to come to me. I protected myself by thinking they'd keep me company. Thanks to them I was not entirely alone and I could let myself go a little, detached from my pleasure. What

I really was, what I wanted to be, I didn't allow them to see, I hid from them. Today, I'm paying the price. Before, I was indifferent to them—or so I thought, at any rate; now I'm beginning to hate them.

If Antoine and I are different now, it's because we have allowed ourselves to be led astray, we've allowed strangers to enter our lives, to transform what we were. I used love and I abused it, believing that I could belong to others. I didn't keep myself for him. My body no longer belongs to me. It has been touched by men I didn't love, it has received from them caresses and pleasure. And now I can't shake off all those memories. Antoine is no longer the only one, the first one, he repeats words already said by others, he sees me in the morning as others used to see me, I smile at him the way I smiled at others, I greet him, I kiss him like the others.

London, 24 August 2001

Sometimes I wonder what would have happened if I hadn't left him after the business with his colleague. I could have swallowed my shame, my anger, and we would have settled peacefully into a calm existence, gradually appeased after the shock of the first betrayal. But I could never have accepted such a life. I would have gone on being angry with him. I might have tried to cheat on him out of spite, out of despair. And then, realizing that I would never be able to forget, to trust him again, I'd have left.

But seeing Antoine again after nearly ten years changed everything. I realized that he still cared about me, that he was prepared to start again. And it was clear that I had no chance of happiness without him.

What I have to do is stop wanting to repeat the past, learn to love him as if he were a stranger. But I can't do it—I have the feeling that we've been robbed of what we had. I persist in thinking that if only there'd been no one during those nine years, everything could have started again as it was in the past. The true betrayal is not to have been with other men, it's having believed that I could be happy with them. At the time I thought that I could live without Antoine—and he too, certainly, must have made plans with other women. And that's why our lives no longer fit together, why they are now dislocated, dispersed. Antoine and I look at one another and we don't recognize ourselves. In our eyes there are always memories lying in wait, threatening to resurface at the first opportunity: a café terrace where Nathalie and Antoine were in the habit of sitting, a bouquet of lilies that reminds me of the flowers Alain used to send.

Those men, those women have marked our lives; it can't be helped. Some of the tracks they've left are superficial: a few expressions here, a few habits there, a particular way of making coffee, of folding clothes. But most of the transformations they've brought about in us are invisible and profound. Sometimes we're not even aware of them. Who knows to what degree his eyes have been shaped by temptations he doesn't even remember, who knows what his caresses on my body owe to the pleasure that he learned to give to others?

Sometimes I feel so bitter, so helpless, that I start to hate them all. I'm angry with them for coming between us, I'm angry with them for having existed. They rise up before me like sentinels who forbid me to go back to the first Antoine—the one I've dreamed of, whom to some degree I invented. I know that's all absurd but I can't help it. There are times when I can't even reason with myself.

London, 20 September 2001

This past while Antoine and I have stopped talking so much about the past. After 9/11 Antoine start to read a lot about international politics, and in the evening when he comes home from the office, all we talk about is the so-called clash of civilizations, the new dangers weighing on democratic regimes and the imminence of an attack on Afghanistan. By moving us away from our memories, these conversations, strangely, have brought the two of us a little closer.

London, 3 October 2001

I've been feeling better in recent days. I walk a lot. I go to galleries, buy books. I've decided to resume studying art history. I've enrolled at the Courtauld Institute. I start in three weeks.

*

It was eleven p.m. Sitting in a corner of Henry J. Bean's pub on King's Road, Antoine was watching Judith sip a gin and tonic. She wasn't used to drinking and after each little sip she winced—it made Antoine smile; maybe she was overdoing it a little. For a while now he had seemed less preoccupied. Judith's jealousy was still a matter of concern—he didn't mention his occasional lunches with Séverine, whom he called only from the office—but they had stopped talking about their pasts.

Antoine told, without enthusiasm, stories from the office, but his attention was elsewhere, on the other side of the pub. When his gaze came back to Judith's face it was too late. A young woman in her late twenties was approaching their table, smiling. Her heavy, athletic legs, her bosom that was already drooping a little under her black sequined top, contrasted with a gentle, round face with a turned-up nose and a pointed chin. Judith noticed that she squinted slightly, which made her look like a little lost girl, embarrassed perhaps by a mature woman's heavy body.

"Antoine! What are you doing here? I was thinking about you just now, telling myself I should have called you, but I was snowed under at work. Ever since I've been in London I haven't stopped running . . ." She spoke hurriedly, sputtering a little and moving her hands a lot. Antoine, ill at ease, was looking at her, dazed. If he'd had his wits about him he might have been able to claim some emergency and make a quick getaway. But he felt Judith's inquisitive gaze and thought to himself that doing so would only have revived her suspicions. So in a tone that he imagined was detached or even indifferent, he said, "That doesn't matter at all, I understand completely . . . Let me introduce Judith. Judith, Kate, a former colleague . . ."

Intrigued, Judith invited her to sit down. Kate protested. "No, that's nice of you, I don't want to disturb you, and anyway, I have to leave."

"Stay for a minute. Just have a drink with us," Judith urged, in the suddenly amiable tone of a saleswoman who realizes that she's about to lose a good customer.

"All right, but just one. I don't want to miss the last train."

Grudgingly, Antoine ordered a bottle of wine. He glared at Judith, furious, but she seemed unaware. She was only interested in Kate.

"Tell me, how long have you been in London?"

"A little over a year. I was living in Paris before..."

"Is that where you met Antoine?"

"Yes, we worked in the same bank."

Turning towards Antoine, hesitant, "That must have been what, a good ten years ago?"

"Around that," Antoine muttered, staring at the toes of his shoes.

"It's funny," said Judith, intending her words for Antoine but not looking at him, "you've never mentioned Kate to me."

As if she wanted to protect him, Kate didn't give Antoine time to react and hastened to reply. "No, but it's not surprising . . . we were just colleagues, that's all."

At what precise moment did the thought lodge itself in Judith's head that this Kate person might be the colleague Antoine had spent a night with nine years ago? Judith herself probably wasn't aware of it. She thought she remembered Antoine mentioning the woman's name at the time, but she wasn't absolutely sure. In fact, it was Antoine's attitude that had roused her suspicion. Seeing him suddenly turn red, stammer more than usual, look around nervously like a turtledove sensing an imminent danger, Judith had a hunch that this woman was more than a mere acquaintance.

The more Judith listened, the more her doubts were confirmed. She should have hated Kate, found her ugly and stupid and of no interest. On the contrary, though, her attention was held only by what a man would almost inevitably find attractive about her: her gentle, moist eyes that seemed at any moment ready to burst into tears; her fleshy lips, her nose which was too small for her face, but gave her an impish look; her slight English accent that made her voice dance at the ends of sentences and gave the impression she was about to choke every time she pronounced the letter *r*.

Antoine watched them chatter while pretending that his mind was elsewhere. He wasn't used to seeing Judith so animated. She seemed interested in everything Kate had to say; she smiled at her, responded, laughing, to her jokes as if she were a childhood friend. Antoine poured each of them another glass of wine, then served himself. He'd never seen Judith intoxicated and he noticed with curiosity how the wine was making her laugh louder and gave her eyes a rebellious and rash expression. He too felt light. The wine had placed between the women and him an invisible barrier that enveloped him, lifted him up, made him feel as if he were floating, invulnerable, disconnected from his life.

Absorbed in his daydream he looked at Kate. She was fiddling nervously with her hair, curling and uncurling the same lock around her index finger. He tried to remember what she'd looked like when he met her. She had probably changed a lot, but he couldn't say how. After all, they'd spent only a night together and immediately afterwards he had tried to erase her and everything about her from his memory. The memory had lingered though. Especially the fear, the feeling of guilt that had followed.

It had happened six months after meeting Judith, in February 1992. Nearly every week Kate came down to the floor where Antoine worked to chat with one of his colleagues. Antoine's office wasn't far from the elevator and every time Kate walked past him they exchanged a smile. How had it started? Who had smiled first? He wasn't sure. They went on because stopping would have been like a signal, as if they realized they'd given the smiles more significance than they should have. One night when Judith was studying at home to prepare for an exam the following day, Antoine had taken advantage of it to stay at the office and catch up on some work. When he finally decided to leave, it was after eleven. There wasn't a soul on his floor. He got into the elevator and to his great surprise Kate was there. She obviously hadn't expected to see him. They smiled their usual smiles and they could perhaps have left it there. But Antoine, without really thinking, invited her for a drink. Why? He still didn't know. Was it because he felt sorry for her with her unruly hair, her heavy ankles, and the shadows under her eyes? Maybe he'd been attracted to the idea of experiencing a moment that would remain forever on the fringe of his life, that wouldn't count, that would engage only a very small part of him? Or maybe he quite simply sensed that she wouldn't turn him down.

And indeed she said yes, without hesitation, without trying to give him the impression that he was behaving boldly. He didn't even know her name.

*

London, 6 October 2001

Antoine, the first time. I was in love with him and with everything that was him. In love with his eyes and his hands. In love with his smile. In love with hearing him say that he loved me. In love with the smell of his neck in bed at night. In love with the kiss he would give me in the morning when he thought I was still asleep. In love with his tired voice on the phone when he stayed late at the office. In love with the sound of his footsteps in the corridor when I'd given up hope that he would come. I was in love with the slightest details of his life. In love with finding out that he loved raspberries and hated asparagus. In love with seeing him wear a cap that didn't suit him at all. In love with the books he read, with the music he liked, his guitar. In love with his fine, erratic handwriting. In love with his accent in English. In love with the way he pronounced my name in French: *Djudith*.

*

Hastily, Kate looked at her watch. "Sorry, must run or I'll miss the last train."

"I'm afraid you already have," said Antoine in a thick voice.

He slowly straightened up, set his glass on the table and while he was staring at the floor, said rather plaintively, "I'd have driven you home, you know, but . . . I don't think I'm in any shape for driving."

"Not at all, I understand," Kate replied. "Don't worry, I'll take a taxi."

Antoine paid the bill and the three stood up. They were staggering slightly, especially Judith. Twice, Antoine had to hold on to her so she wouldn't bump into the tables.

Outside, it was raining. They stood at the corner of the street, waiting for a taxi, but there was none to be seen. "This always happens in London," Antoine muttered. "A few drops of rain and you can't find a taxi!" And he began to gripe, his jacket over his head to protect himself from the rain.

"Go home," said Kate. "Don't worry about me, I'll find a taxi."

Antoine was tempted to obey her and leave her there, but Judith held him back.

"No, no, we aren't going to leave you all alone at this time of night! Why don't you stay over at our place? We're not far from here..."

And fearing Antoine's reaction she glanced at him out of the corner of her eye. He didn't say a word, had even stopped complaining. But she knew from the look on his face that he was furious.

When they arrived, Antoine went straight to the bedroom and shut the door. Judith opened the sofa bed in the living room, gave Kate sheets and a bath towel.

In the bedroom, Antoine, already in pyjamas, was pacing as he waited for her. He exploded.

"What got into you, inviting her here to sleep?"

"Nothing, I . . ."

"What are you up to anyway?"

Judith was taken aback.

"I don't understand, Antoine. I just wanted to be kind to her. After all, she's your friend . . ."

"She's not my friend!" Antoine exclaimed.

He didn't even try to lower his voice.

"Ssshh! She'll hear you!"

"I don't care! This is my home. I don't know what you're trying to prove by inviting her here but whatever it is I want her out tomorrow morning. Good night!"

He switched off the light, lay down and pulled the covers over his head. Judith groped her way to the bed, sat up for a moment, then laid her head on her pillow. A ray of light threaded its way under the door. She could hear Kate pacing the living room as if she'd lost something. Judith was intrigued by her. She would have liked to know more about her life, her past, her plans. In particular she'd have liked to understand how Antoine could have been attracted to her.

The living-room lamp was still on. Judith got up and silently left the bedroom. She tiptoed down the hall and stopped at the door to the living room. Kate was sitting on the sofa, leafing through a magazine.

"Aren't you tired?" said Judith, approaching her.

Kate looked up at her. She seemed a little surprised.

"No, when I drink too much I have trouble sleeping."

"Me too. Would you like a tisane? That might help."

"Yes, I would. That's sweet of you."

Judith went to the kitchen and came back a few minutes later with two cups of verveine. She sat down next to Kate on the sofa.

"Antoine looks a little tired," Kate said.

"Yes, he has a lot of work."

"He's preoccupied . . ."

"Yes, I think he is. Was he very different when you knew him?"

"No . . . I don't know. I didn't know him all that well."

"You don't have to explain, I understand."

Kate gave Judith a quizzical look. Judith smiled as if to reassure her. She went on. "I assume there was something between you."

"Yes, but it was just one night. After that he had no interest in me."

"Why?"

"I don't know . . . I think there must have been someone else."

"And you didn't try to see him again?"

"No, why bother? When I ran into him by chance a year ago he was very cordial, even offered to help me find an apartment, but he never mentioned what had gone on between us. I think he saw it as something foolish."

Her broad face darkened. Looking up at Judith she asked, "What about you, have you known Antoine for a long time?"

"Yes . . . but we've only been together since . . ."

She didn't have time to finish. Antoine had come into the living room without a sound and was standing in front of them, arms dangling, his expression threatening. He swayed slightly, like a man absorbed in prayer. His eyes, bloodshot and with dark rings, seemed to be staring at the window behind them. Two deep wrinkles drew a large V on his forehead. Judith had never seen him in this state.

Suddenly he started moving, like an old machine that's finally been fixed, and murmured, barely holding back his rage, "What are you two up to?" Judith and Kate dared not look at one another. They stayed on the sofa, frozen, their eyes turned towards Antoine. "What are you two cooking up?" he repeated. His voice was hoarse and thick, still weighed down by wine. "I've had just about enough, I mean it!"

Judith stood up, took his hand, tried to calm him down. "Come on, Antoine, let's go back to bed, we've had too much to drink, we need a good night's sleep..." But he pushed her away, violently. His hands were shaking, he was gasping for breath. Speaking to Judith, as if Kate didn't exist, "I don't want her here! Send her away! She can go to a hotel, I'll pay for the room, it makes no difference to me." Judith went up to him again. "Please, Antoine, you don't know what you're saying... It's my fault, it's all my fault, so please, come back to bed..." But Antoine pushed away her arm even more brutally. He turned towards Kate and muttered through clenched teeth, "What were you telling her about, eh?" Kate looked him in the eyes without replying. "What exactly did you tell her anyway?" Keeping her eyes on him, Kate finally got up. She was smiling, her smile ingenuous, nearly loving. But her disarming tenderness made Antoine even more furious. He went up to her, grabbed her by the shoulders and, pushing his face close to hers, muttered, his mouth taut with anger, "Go away now and leave us alone!" Kate still hadn't moved, she had the same smile, the same gentle expression. Antoine grabbed her by the arm and dragging her to the door, opened it and pushed her violently onto the staircase. She stumbled, fell, landed on her arm, then tumbled headfirst to the bottom.

*

London, 8 October 2001

I woke with a start. I hadn't felt such anxiety for a long time.

It often happened when I was a child. A kind of rubber ball. At first it stayed in my hand. Then it began to swell. Slowly at first, imperceptibly, then faster and faster. And I watch it grow, stretch, spread. I try to hold it back, to contain it. But there's nothing to be done, it keeps spreading, driven by an inner strength, inexorable. Finally, it wraps itself around me, covers my arms, my chest, my face. It fills all the space, it blocks the horizon. It's like birdlime, with no colour, no smell or taste, a cold magma that sticks to me, that penetrates my body. Now I can't move, I panic, but the more I resist the more the thing tightens its grip. Submerged by the immense mass, I become very small, I feel my skin contract, my blood rushes back to my heart, I am merely a minuscule dot, lost, about to disappear. Then suddenly something happens, everything topples and I start to grow again. Now I'm the one who is swelling and inflating, I stretch, I open, I spread out, dilate, I become a giant, bloated, puffed up. I have become the thing. I'm torn apart, carried away in the vastness. My arms, my legs, I can't make them stop, they extend as far as the eye can see. And beyond the body that is carrying me away, I catch a glimpse of the emptiness that I must fill. I'd like to stop, slow down the reckless flight, but the more I resist the more I am hurled into my fall. I feel dizzy, suddenly weak, then finally I stop wanting, I accept everything. And that is when, little by little, the symptoms are finally smoothed away, the dark horizon reappears and I wake up, drained of all my strength.

*

Antoine was standing, gasping and dazed, at the top of the stairs. Judith elbowed him aside and went down. At the bottom of the stairs she came to a brief standstill in front of Kate's inert body. Then, slowly, she approached, as if it was an injured animal whose ultimate attack she feared. Kate seemed to be asleep.

Judith tapped her cheeks. No reaction. She turned her over, stretched her out on her side, shook her. Still nothing. She tried to lift Kate's head. That was when she saw a drop of blood at the corner of her lips.

Judith shrank back, scared, as if afraid that by touching this body its stillness would somehow be passed on to her. Antoine joined Judith at the bottom of the stairs. He too began to shake Kate, to try as best he could to take her pulse, to see if her heart was still beating. Behind him he heard Judith's muffled voice, "Antoine, please, do something." He did not reply. Kneeling before the body, hands on his thighs, he didn't move. Judith wondered if he was paralyzed by fear or simply indifferent, unable to understand what had really happened. Standing behind him, she repeated, panicking, "Antoine, we have to do something!" Finally, Antoine got up and leaned against the door. "There's nothing we can do. It's too late."

4

Exelmans Station, Paris, 12 October 2002

It's eleven-thirty p.m. Benoît Joubert is happy. His daughter, Hélène, has just found out that she's admitted to the École de médecine! His daughter, his own daughter, a doctor! How proud his mother would have been! During his lunch hour he bought champagne and flowers. Hélène had promised to wait up for him and have a drink before she went to bed. He is approaching Exelmans station. Now just four more stops till the terminus. From there he'll take a taxi so he won't waste any time.

Every time he arrives at Exelmans station, Benoît is a little nervous. Sitting in his cab, he keeps his foot firmly on the brake pedal. He slows down more than usual. The others say that it never happens twice in the same station, but that's exactly what he's afraid of. These things always happen to him and never to anyone else. He sees again the man in a striped suit standing on the platform. His face is blank. His gaze betrays no emotion, neither anger nor dread nor despair. And yet, as Benoît was approaching the station, he had detected something about the man. For a second he had sensed that the man wanted to die—that in a way he'd already departed this earth. That perhaps that was the reason why his expression was so blank, so naked. Suddenly, the man who resembled an apparition had jumped in front of the train. That was three years ago. Since then, whenever he arrives at Exelmans station, Benoît is vigilant, his hands are tight on the levers, his foot on the pedal, ready to brake.

On the night in question there is just one person in the station, a man in his forties. He is standing on the platform, reading his newspaper. Benoît smiles and, relieved, closes his eyes for a moment. The man is not the suicidal type. This time, nothing will happen, definitely. Suddenly though, a young man emerges from the shadows, rushes at the man with the newspaper, arms outstretched before him. The man's back is turned; he doesn't even see him. The young man pushes him in front of the train. Benoît slams on the brake. Too late. A few seconds later the train stops. Mechanically, Benoît turns off the ignition and sits there, still, dazed. His hands, gripping his knees, are shaking. He has trouble breathing. He looks at the lilies he bought for Hélène, scattered over the floor of the cab. His foot hasn't left the brake pedal. He continues to press with all his might. A gnawing, cold pain that starts at his heel climbs slowly up the length of his leg. It spreads, stretches, it reaches his knee, his thigh, it clears a path to his heart, like a prelude to death.

*

Paris, 21 November 2002

Here I am again, alone. I don't yet realize how much my life has been transformed. It's been more than a year since Kate's death turned my life upside down.

I know that I lost everything, but I'm not yet aware of it. Maybe that's why I can still find the strength to write. To avoid keeling over, to remain whole, but also to prepare myself, to learn how to love my solitude.

I reread some pages from my journal this morning. Leaving New York, meeting Antoine again, our happiness, our jealousy. I told myself that it would help me understand how it all started. The violence, the determination I would never have believed I had in me. But maybe I shouldn't try so hard to find explanations. Maybe I should be content to tell my stories as if they weren't from my own life.

Reasons, motives there surely are, there always are. But what good is it to rack my brain looking for them? To tell myself that it could have been otherwise, that we could have chosen another route, that we could have found within us the strength to step back while there was still time? And maybe after Kate's death we could have . . . could have what? Called the police, explained the accident? Antoine might have got off with a ten-year sentence. But that would have required us to still be capable of reasoning. Above all, we'd have had to agree to no longer be together.

*

Judith watched Antoine. His movements were slow and precise, as if he had long since been ready for this task. He'd gone to get a big rug from the guest room and laid it on the floor. After wrapping the body in garbage bags he placed it at one end of the rug and rolled it up inside. Judith watched while he carefully tied the rug up with a rope. She dared not ask any questions.

When he finished, he looked up at Judith. "I'll need your help loading it into the car."

*

Paris, 24 November 2002

This morning, I went out. It was cold and the brisk air filled with all sorts of autumnal smells felt good. I went to the market, bought fruit and fish. I even exchanged a few words with the fish-seller, who recognized me. "It's been a while since we've seen you, I hope you haven't been sick," she said. I explained that I'd been away on vacation, a sabbatical, and the words came out of my mouth as if they were true. What's more, she seemed to believe me. "Ah, yes, I know what you mean! It's good to have a change of air. Anyway, I'm glad to see you!" I felt so grateful, I wanted to say something pleasant to her but I couldn't think of anything, so I just smiled, thinking that there is no greater joy in the world than to feel ordinary, a person like everyone else, lost in the benevolent mass of humankind.

*

In the car they had to bow their heads a little because of the rug, which nearly touched the windshield. Judith was driving. As she didn't know London well, Antoine was guiding her. To avoid being noticed they took the small streets behind King's Road to Battersea Bridge. Now and then Judith would look at Antoine from the corner of her eye. The light from the streetlamps slipped onto his face, so that he looked by turns gloomy and peaceful, gentle and agitated, vigorous and old. She no longer even asked him what was on his mind. She was too afraid of his reaction. She was content to follow his instructions—barely inaudible grunts that he sometimes accompanied with waving arms. Past Battersea Bridge, they drove along the Thames towards Chelsea Harbour, stopped on a small street that led to the wharf and got out of the car. The neighbourhood was deserted. All that could be heard were the water lapping against the bank and the distant hum of traffic. On the Battersea Bridge side, a bluish glimmer was spreading above the city fog. They headed back to the car. It was barely twenty metres to the wharves. Judith helped Antoine take the carpet out and drag it to the bank. They took a last look around them, then pushed it into the river. Gliding against the stone, the carpet made a sound like a zipper being hastily opened. A long moment passed and finally they heard a splash. Kneeling at the edge of the wharf they leaned over towards the river: five metres down, the carpet was slowly sinking into the water.

*

Paris, 26 November 2002

In the days following Kate's death we stayed inside Antoine's apartment. He had resigned from the bank, claiming "family problems." He was transformed. He paced the sitting room, unable to sit for more than five minutes, and heaved long, plaintive sighs. When I spoke to him he would look at me, bewildered, as if he didn't know who I was, or as if I'd just delivered some irreparable insult. He almost never answered my questions.

Though he was usually so serene, so much in control of his emotions, his inner life now seemed suddenly to have accumulated on the surface of his body: he wrung his hands with dread, bit his nails, jumped at the slightest sound, grimaced every time the phone rang. Tics had even appeared: the corner of his mouth would contract, as if shaken by an electrical charge, and at any moment he would shrug his shoulders as if something inside him was trying to say, "It's nothing, all that. Everyone has to die one day. And that's only the beginning of death."

Mornings, he often felt nauseous and would spend fifteen minutes in the bathroom, vomiting—almost nothing but bile. Then he would fix himself some coffee (he boiled it in a saucepan, very finely ground, with sugar and cinnamon). It was, he maintained, the only thing he could get down. Around nine o'clock he would go out for the newspapers. He bought them all, even the neighbourhood ones. Back inside, he would leaf through them eagerly, systematically, not lingering over any piece of news, simply wanting to know if Kate's death had been reported and what they had to say about it.

At night I would hear him grinding his teeth. Sometimes he moaned, murmuring confused words in his sleep, drawing up complicated plans. He would say my name too, his voice impatient and panicky, urgent. I tried to calm him down but as soon as I touched him he would wake with a start, wild-eyed, sweating.

*

The two of them are sitting in the kitchen. For some months now they've been avoiding the sitting room. The window looks out on the street and the murmur of the city is a constant reminder that they are no longer part of this world, that they no longer have a place in it. Antoine forces himself to eat a slice of bread. The night before, he was having dizzy spells again. Judith was right; he needs to get his strength back. She doesn't look at him. He seems aloof, indifferent to her and to her fear. She tells herself that anxiety can't be shared. She thinks about death. The only way out would be to die together. But she says nothing to him. It's not yet time.

Later that night they will wake up at almost the same time. Unable to get back to sleep they'll wait, looking up at the ceiling where the pale lights from the street will stretch out. Ambulance sirens, cries, the laughter of passersby will startle them, in unison. Their hands will seek each other, will join feverishly and stay like that, motionless, for a very long moment. But that embrace brings them no comfort.

Then Judith will turn to Antoine, without looking at him. She will sit on his belly and after she takes off her nightgown, she will lean towards him and bring her bosom close to his face. Then slowly, methodically, she will help him enter her and they'll make love with their eyes closed, without a sound, seeking only their own pleasure and, after pleasure, sleep.

*

Paris, 27 November 2002

The body was found a month later, near Battersea Bridge. According to the papers, a man who'd gone onto the riverbank to retrieve a key had discovered it.

I think that Antoine was relieved at first. She'd finally been found, that was one less uncertainty. Soon, though, other questions began to torment him: there would certainly be an inquest and by searching, they would be bound to discover the truth. As if he himself was trying to prove his guilt, he would draw up all sorts of scenarios that would put the investigators on the right trail: someone might have seen them talking to Kate at Henry J. Bean's, or on King's Road when they were waiting for a taxi. Perhaps his neighbours had seen the three of them come in that night. Or some lingering reveller had spotted them loading the carpet into the car.

Antoine was convinced that someone would find them, that it was just a matter of time. He so feared being recognized that he refused to go out by himself. I had to go with him everywhere. He told himself that a couple was less likely to arouse suspicions than a man on his own.

Most of the time I was the one who answered the phone. Fortunately, it rang less and less often. Our few friends hardly called us at all. Sometimes on weekends a woman would call and ask to speak to Antoine without wanting to give her name. I was sure it was Nathalie. He never talked to her for very long. I could hear him whispering anxiously. He seemed annoyed that she kept calling, and that set my mind at rest.

I shared Antoine's anxiety all the more because I was afraid of losing him. I could have encouraged him to give himself up to the police. He would have explained that it had been an accident, I'd have supported him and if they believed us, he might have been sentenced to a few years in jail for manslaughter.

But I knew that the thought of ending up in prison terrified him. For him it meant the end of everything. He preferred to count on the hope, no matter how faint, that he would never be discovered. For the time being he lived in the constant terror of being arrested, but after a few years his fear would finally go and he might go back to a nearly normal life.

*

"Name?"

"Antoine Lemercier."

"Address?"

"34a Flood Street."

"Occupation?"

"Financial analyst."

The inspector, a man in his forties, tall and well-padded, was looking calmly at Antoine. His piggy little deep-set eyes seemed about to disappear, submerged in the fat that puffed up the rest of his face. The other man, younger but already portly, was taking notes, now and then looking up at Antoine. They'd arrived around noon with no warning. The inspector had presented his badge to Antoine and courteously, practically apologetically, explained that his name was in the address book of a woman named Kate Waterton, whose body had been found some weeks before. As a special investigation was under way, he had to question everyone who'd known Ms. Waterton even slightly.

Antoine had invited them to sit in the dining room. He'd even been about to offer them tea but at the last minute changed his mind, reckoning that he mustn't try too hard to appear relaxed. In any case, he didn't need to make efforts. He had anticipated this moment for so long, rehearsed the scenario about the interrogation in his head so many times, in so many forms, that he felt safe from any surprise. Even more, he was so firmly convinced that he would eventually be arrested that he had no trouble lying.

"Did you know that Ms. Waterton was dead?"

"Yes, I read about it in the paper."

"How did you know her?"

"I met her in Paris around ten years ago. We worked together."

"Did you see her outside of work?"

"No."

"How do you explain that your name appears in her address book?"

"I saw her again briefly last year. She'd just moved to London and she asked me to help her find an apartment."

The inspector smiled and looked at his colleague out of the corner of his eye. He went on.

"Have you seen her since then?"

"No."

"Where were you on the night of October 8?"

"I'm not sure . . . May I look in my datebook?"

"Go ahead."

Antoine went into the kitchen and came back with a notebook bound in grey leather. He turned the pages, pretended to be thinking, as if he really were trying to give a precise answer.

"I must have been at home. Here, see for yourself."

The inspector took the datebook, leafed through it, frowning slightly, and gave it back. He turned to his colleague, who still had his nose in his note pad.

"Is there anything else? Have I forgotten anything?"

"No. I'm sure that's everything. For now."

After they left, Antoine was relieved. But the interrogation had opened a new world of doubts and questions for him. He had trouble believing that they knew so little about Kate's death. It seemed incredible that they hadn't even hinted at what caused it. Of course, it all might have been part of some ploy to trap him, to make him say more than he claimed to know. The exaggerated politeness, the easygoing tone of voice, the gentle, nearly compassionate smiles weren't those of a policeman on a routine job. Antoine suspected that before the interrogation the inspector must have informed himself about his life, his past. He might even have talked to his neighbours and his former colleagues. In any event, Antoine was sure they'd be back. They were just getting started.

*

Paris, 29 November 2002

A few weeks later two police inspectors came to call on Antoine. It must have been around noon. I was in the bedroom tidying up. Before he opened the door, Antoine came and told me to stay put and not make a sound. He didn't want me to get involved. I sat on the floor beside the door and waited.

I remember I could feel my heart beating very hard. I was afraid I'd pass out and attract their attention.

I listened to them talking, the inspector's calm voice and kindly tone, Antoine's replies, his voice a little hesitant. I told myself that they might arrest him, that I would be alone, not knowing what was going to happen to him, unable to talk to him. I remember the hatred that I felt for those two men. I pictured their ironic smiles, their expressions full of insinuations. In their eyes there was—I was nearly sure of it—the violent and haughty pleasure of hunters who calmly watch as their dogs encircle a fox. They were only doing their job, of course, but every one of their questions sounded to me like a trap for Antoine to fall into, and each of their silent reactions a sign that they were seeing their doubts confirmed.

When they finally left, I opened the bedroom door. I would have liked Antoine to put his arms around me. But he was slumped in an easy chair, elbows on his knees, hands on his face. Fear, which had loosened its grip a little over the past few days, had come back immediately, with its trail of speculations, uncertainties and unanswered questions. It was as if our isolation had given our lives some of the texture of dreams, so much so that we weren't sure if Kate really was dead, if the months of anxiety we'd just gone through hadn't been some fiction we'd imagined until the policemen's visit suddenly brought us back to reality.

I took a few steps towards Antoine. I no longer knew how to get through to him, how to reach him. I knelt beside his chair and began to stroke his head. I could hear his breathing, heavy, practically a gasp. For some time it was as if he were wearing a mask. Anxiety had engraved on his forehead wrinkles so deep and tinted his eyes with a gleam so grim-looking that his face seemed devoid of all expression, like a faded portrait whose outlines you can no longer make out. Then he straightened up and without even looking at me took my head in his hands, kissed my fevered brow and pushed me away almost at once, as if the emotions that were controlling him had immediately gained the upper hand, never letting him get away from himself for very long.

Paris, 30 November 2002

The months that followed brought little change. Antoine had become very dependent on me. Since the inspectors' visit he'd refused to go out during the daytime. I was the one who did the shopping, and he even gave me the job of buying the papers.

We didn't talk very much—we no longer had anything to learn from one another. We were living with the same fear, the same helplessness. We no longer took pleasure in being together, but we couldn't stand to be separated. Antoine needed in particular to feel that I was constantly at his side. If I took longer than usual to buy groceries he'd call me on my cellphone, his voice anxious and filled with reproaches. When I stayed in the bathroom longer than usual I would hear him prowling behind the door; I pictured him with ears pricked to check that I really was inside, to make sure that nothing had happened to me.

Antoine had moments of lightness too. Reading the paper he would sometimes land on a story that cheered him up—a celebrity divorced a month after the wedding, a member of the royal family caught enthusiastically shaking hands with an old dictator—and that would give us a chance to forget ourselves a little by talking about others. Sometimes too we talked about travel. "I'd like to go to Iceland, or Alaska, somewhere cold where there aren't many people." I encouraged him, got brochures we'd leaf through together in the evening lying in bed. But these enthusiasms never lasted very long. His face would darken and I could tell from his expression that he was no longer able to see a future for himself. He was able briefly to escape, to slip like a burglar into the territory of dreams, but he soon realized that he no longer had a place there.

*

Antoine waited till Judith had gone out to buy groceries before he called Séverine. At first, all he wanted was to hear her voice. It seemed to him as if that alone would comfort him. He remembered their conversations in Cannes some years earlier. Séverine would definitely reassure him, even if he didn't always listen to what she said. Séverine was so completely in command of herself and of her life, and since he often felt that he no longer had any control over his own, her serenity restored his confidence.

He listened to Séverine talk about how she spent her days, running from one place to another: home to daycare, daycare to office, office to supermarket, supermarket to daycare... Antoine couldn't concentrate on what she was saying, but he let himself be lulled by the sound of her voice, adding occasionally, "Yes... I understand...." simply to let Séverine know he was still there and encourage her to go on. Her voice, at once weary and cheerful, reminded Antoine that life could be something other than the anxiety and terror that now enveloped every moment of his existence.

But soon another voice—a strange and desperate voice—could be heard inside him. It was a muted but determined voice that he could not silence, a voice that was saying, "You know, Séverine, things are bad, really bad. Something happened. I . . . I . . ." Little by little the voice got louder. The more Antoine tried to stifle it, the more it rose and grew inside him. It became more and more strident; it was becoming a howl that soon he wouldn't be able to hold in. Séverine, at the other end, was still talking about her children. One, the youngest, surely, had started to shriek. He was asking for his mother, tugging her, claiming that his sister had hit him. Séverine apologized to Antoine and promised to call him back later. Antoine hung up, relieved. Long afterwards, though, the voice kept murmuring inside him. "Séverine, something happened. I . . . she's dead . . . she's dead."

*

Paris, 2 December 2002

Ordinary couples end up resembling one another. Each person rubs off on the other because they are sure that nothing will separate them. Out of love, out of necessity above all, they come to use the same expressions, to answer the phone the same way, to like the same music, to complain about the same ills. The difference, which in the beginning sharpens feelings, eventually irritates, so they neutralize it, making everyday life more bearable. For Antoine and me it was the reverse. It wasn't the certainty of a life together but the constant anxiety about being separated that had brought us closer, that made each of us unconsciously mimic the existence of the other. Being able to guess what frightened him, what annoyed him, what gave him, for a brief moment, reason to hope, was a way to keep him close to me and also to slow down my fall, as I felt there was now nothing solid around me I could hang onto.

Paris, 6 December 2002

Around the end of February I got a letter from my Paris landlord. He wanted to take over the apartment and was asking me to remove my belongings. I didn't have much, some clothes and books mainly, but there were also Dad's photos, which were very important to me.

When I suggested going to Paris, Antoine seemed surprised. I sensed that he wanted to, but I also knew that he would say no. Nonetheless, I did all I could to persuade him: it would be good for us both, it would give us a break, we'd be able to go walking together without the constant fear of being recognized. Antoine, though, was terrified at the thought of leaving his apartment. It was irrational and he knew it: if they'd wanted to arrest him or question him again, they didn't have to wait for him to leave his place. And even if the police were having him watched, there was nothing compromising about spending a few days in Paris.

He was afraid of staying alone too, but I assured him I'd only be gone for three nights. I rented a big car and to avoid saying goodbye, I got on the road very early in the morning. During the night he snuggled up to me more than usual, as if he were trying to store up some affection. It was quite elementary—a raw need to feel another body, to touch living matter.

I got to Paris around three in the afternoon. I parked near the apartment, but instead of going there immediately, I went for a walk. After all those months shut inside with Antoine, I needed to be alone. I was so used to his presence that without him, I felt myself become another person. Finally, I could let my thoughts roam freely. I'd forgotten how much I love browsing in bookstores, checking out boutiques, watching the passing crowd. I stopped feeling guilty about being in Paris without Antoine. I thought about him now and then, but I didn't mind his not being there.

At night I went to a bistro near the Odéon and ordered a *steak frites*. The aroma of grilled meat, the taste of blood in my mouth made me rediscover sensations with newfound intensity. Suddenly I felt confident, eager to receive within me all the rediscovered abundance of the world. A man in his forties a few tables away kept giving me furtive glances. Brown hair, tall, close-shaven, he was also eating heartily. Across from him was an older man, perhaps his father. He got up from the table, most likely to go to the men's room. The younger man's gaze settled on me insistently. I waited for him to smile at me, inviting me to join them—and if he had, I think I'd have accepted. But the other man came back and they resumed their conversation. When I left the bistro I passed very close to their table, brushing his shoulder. He didn't look up, but I could sense his gaze behind my back. And it reassured me to tell myself that the man had nearly spoken to me, that if I'd really wanted it, it could have been the start of something new.

When I got to the apartment it must have been around nine-thirty. The first thing I did was call Antoine. His voice seemed more lugubrious than usual. Maybe because I felt so light myself since I'd left London. He didn't seem interested in what I told him. All he wanted was to know when I'd be back—I had to remind him over and over that I was spending three nights in Paris.

Then I climbed into bed. To help me get to sleep I touched myself. It was the first time since I'd been with Antoine.

*

It was around five o'clock. Antoine had woken up late—it was his first night in months without Judith. He went out to buy the papers and sat in the kitchen and ate a soft-boiled egg.

When the doorbell rang he jumped. He even felt a small shiver run down his back. His right hand began to shake a little. Stealthily, he walked to the front door. He looked out the spy hole. It was Nathalie.

Antoine heaved a long sigh. He went on observing her. A moment later she rang again. She had on a black wool coat, fitted at the waist. She rummaged in her purse—a famous brand, needless to say—and took out a pocket mirror. She began to inspect her face nervously, brushing her cheeks with her fingertips, pressing her lips together the better to apply her lipstick. Her ash-blond hair, freshly coloured, emerged in loose curls from a red wool cap. She was about to take it off, hesitated briefly, then decided not to. Antoine knew it would be best not to open the door. She would wait another few minutes, then leave. That night she might have called him. He wouldn't have answered and that would have been the end of it. But seeing her there on the doorstep, elegant and energetic, suddenly filled Antoine with curiosity. He wondered where she was living and with whom. He wondered too how she would react when she saw him. She would certainly see that he'd changed, but would she have any idea about how much his life had been transformed? Maybe she would be so alarmed that she'd try to leave right away. But it's not certain that Antoine really did ask himself those questions. Probably he'd just said: she's away, I'm alone, why not? And he opened the door.

"No kiss? That's not a very warm welcome."

Antoine approached her, placed his hands on her shoulders as if he were trying to keep her there, and kissed her cheeks, careful to keep his mouth away from hers. Then he asked her in.

"You're on your own?" she asked, handing him her coat.

"Yes."

There was some hesitation in his voice. Someone more perceptive would have realized that Antoine was still feeling Judith's presence, but Nathalie didn't allow herself to be distracted by that kind of thought. Without waiting for him to invite her to sit down, she went into the sitting room as if she were mistress of the place and settled on the sofa near the window.

"Aren't you going to offer me a drink?"

Feeling that he'd been caught out, Antoine stammered, "Yes... What can I bring you?"

"Perrier with a little lemon and one ice cube, please."

When Antoine came back he'd pulled himself together somewhat.

"Why have you come here?" he asked, sitting across from her, on the other side of the coffee table.

"Just like that. Aren't you glad to see me?"

"That depends..."

"I wanted to know how you were, that's all. By the way, you look awfully tired," she added, examining Antoine from head to toe.

"Yes, I haven't been getting a lot of sleep recently."

"But I thought you were happy, you and... what's her name, again?"

"Judith."

"Yes, right!" she said, with an ironic smile. "Judith— she hasn't left you, I hope?"

Antoine pretended to ignore her. Then, in the same indifferent, irritated tone, "And you, what are you up to?"

"Not much. I travel, I meet people... But I'm concerned about you," she said, her voice serious. "You don't look well..."

Antoine sighed. He couldn't stand to look her in the eye.

"Look, Nathalie," he said finally. "It's very kind of you to drop in. Now I think it would be best if you left."

Nathalie didn't seem surprised. She got up silently and started for the door. He went with her, holding out her coat. But just as he was about to peck her on the cheeks he let her press her body against him. As she was loosening her embrace she pressed her lips against Antoine's rough cheek and then onto his mouth. Instead of freeing himself, Antoine embraced her in turn and kissed her—awkwardly, almost angrily, as if he were trying to put into it all the violence that he couldn't summon to push her away. Then, unable to stifle his desire, he took her by the hand and dragged her into the bedroom.

*

Paris, 7 December 2002

The next morning I began sorting my papers. In a tin box I found photos: photos of David in a restaurant in New York; a photo of Alain in a striped suit, his eyes sparkling, smile candid, proud and empty; and some photos of Dad. One in particular intrigued me. It was in our apartment on avenue de Suffren. I was sitting at one end of the sofa, Dad at the other. We both had the same serious and worried expression. We hadn't even bothered to smile; we were staring into the distance, apparently at the same point. We gave the impression of suddenly remembering some very important detail or receiving some upsetting news that concerned only us. Or maybe we'd quite simply noticed our own image in the living-room mirror and the photo had captured our astonishment, our sorrow at discovering how sad we looked.

I also discovered the first part of my journal. I started to reread some passages—Dad's death, Alain, meeting Antoine. And I wondered how it was possible to have changed so much in such a short time, practically without noticing.

Paris, 8 December 2002

When I was a child, one of my favourite games was Red Light/Green Light. One child gets to be the stoplight, while the others form a line about four metres away. The stoplight turns her back to the line, facing a tree and says "green light." The children then move towards her, but as soon as she turns around and says "red light," they must stop. Those caught moving have to go back to the starting line.

Rereading my journal, I sometimes feel like that stoplight child, standing against a tree with my whole life bustling behind me. As soon as I turn around, it freezes, only allowing me to see dislocated moments.

Our lives wait until our backs are turned to move ahead. As soon as we observe ourselves, as soon as we stop to take stock of the situation, to weigh the pros and cons, as soon as we question ourselves about our motives, our motivations, our reasons, nothing more happens. Under the searchlights of a mind too greedy to understand, the flow of existence is broken. Life is modest; it refuses to be looked at, scrutinized, analyzed, reduced to a single story. So, as soon as we try to understand it, fit it into a groove, it comes to a standstill, plays dead—and nothing is left before us but scattered bits. How had I been able to force myself to leave Antoine the first time? How did I end up in New York, with men I didn't love who probably only half-loved me? How, after finding Antoine again, had we come to shatter what we'd looked forward to so much? I can go to great lengths to find answers, link together the events, the genuine passages in our lives: the roads

I've taken are still obscure to me. I can recount, retrace the steps; but the substance of life, that links one step with the other, still escapes me. Language creates the illusion of continuity, but that continuity is still without texture, without colour, the meaning that it harbours dense and opaque. The life of the past doesn't like being in the limelight. As soon as it feels examined, it hides away, silent, like a tracked animal. It spies on us and only comes out of the shadows when we're distracted—it's always when our backs are turned that it catches up with us and engulfs us completely.

Paris, 9 December 2002

I came back from Paris a day early. Very quickly I'd stopped sorting. I packed nearly everything, leaving only some old cookbooks, a few pairs of shoes and the small TV. I got on the road around the end of the afternoon. On the boat I started to think about Antoine again. In Paris the night before, I could almost have imagined living without him, but knowing that I'd soon be seeing him again, I realized that I really did miss him. Seeing the lights of Dover, I was more and more excited. I was also afraid that something might have happened to him, that the police had come back, that they'd taken him to the station to interrogate him. I drove very fast in the night and when I got to London it must have been one a.m.

I parked a few metres from home. I was about to get out when I saw our front door open. A young woman dressed in black, with a red cap, appeared and turned back towards the door, smiling, before she went down the stairs. I wondered if I'd made a mistake, if it really was Antoine's house, but as I looked at the woman going down the lane to the metal gate, I recognized in a corner the plastic crates where Antoine stowed old newspapers. There was no doubt: she was coming out of his house. I watched her walk away. Her steps were quick, determined, as if she had just concluded a good deal and was thinking about the cozy bed awaiting her at home. I started the car again and followed her down Flood Street. She turned at the corner. While she was crossing the street she rummaged in her purse, probably in search of her car key. I was just a few metres from her. I floored the gas. We made eye contact for a fraction of a second—just long enough for her to see my face, just long enough for me to make out hers, distorted by fear. There was a big shock, then I braked. I sat there for a moment, as if paralyzed, gasping for breath. I looked up at the rearview mirror. She was lying there, lifeless, in the middle of the road, the contents of her purse scattered around her.

I started up again. I drove without really thinking of where I was going. The streets went by, identical, like endless tunnels of light. From neighbourhood to neighbourhood the same houses, the same garish posters. I didn't even try to remember what route I'd taken; I didn't try to give myself reference points. All that mattered was to get away from that body, to keep driving, as far as I could, as long as I could. I no longer remember the multitude of ideas that passed through my head, but one continued to torment me long afterwards: what if she weren't dead? She'd seen my face, of that I was sure. Maybe she'd be able to describe me to the police?

After an hour or maybe two, I stopped by the side of the road. On my right, a row of Victorian houses; on my left, a dark mass of woods (I realized the next morning that I'd ended up near Hampstead Heath). I locked the doors and lay down on the backseat, knees to my chest, hands under my cheek. As soon as I closed my eyes I saw the scene again, saw her horrified look, her wide-open mouth, frozen in the expression of a scream, but unable to emit the smallest sound, like someone anticipating death. Then the impact, the sound of the body against the bumper, the image of the woman stretched out on the street, inert. At first, I tried to tell myself that someone else had done it, that I'd stayed behind and had been only the helpless executioner of that person's will; then I felt as if I'd become that other person, relinquishing everything to her and becoming nothing more than a dried-out carcass, exiled from human memory. There was only that thing, that moment, that voiceless woman. In my delirium I had become that woman, frozen in horror and unable to cry out; I saw the enormous car, the avalanche of metal, moving towards me. But what frightened me most was the expression of the woman who was driving the car, a terrified look imbued with my own fear.

When I woke up it must have been around six o'clock. The sun was sparkling through the branches of the birch trees. I was still exhausted and my anxiety didn't come back right away, so I could believe for a few seconds that what had happened the night before also belonged to the fringes of sleep. I got out of the car to stretch my legs. When I caught sight of the damaged bumper I felt my fear reawaken. I mustn't stay there, I told myself. I needed to get back on the road at once. I stopped at a gas station to buy a map of London and after several errors I finally found my way to Chelsea. When I turned in the car I explained to the rental agent that I'd lost control of it on a turn and had run into a lamppost. He seemed a little surprised, but merely asked me where and at what time the accident had happened, then gave me a copy of his report.

When I arrived at Antoine's I noticed a police car parked across the street, light flashing. I went inside without a sound and lay down in the sitting room with all my clothes on. A few minutes later I heard Antoine open the bedroom door. He went into the sitting room, eyes still swollen from sleep. I got up, slowly; I walked towards him, looking down, and threw myself into his arms. I remember how good his embrace felt. I stayed for a long time with my head nestled in his neck. I imagined his face, his expression of helplessness when he sensed that I was crying and that there was nothing he could do to understand me, to comfort me.

*

Since her return from Paris, Judith had been transformed. Often Antoine would hear her crying in the bathroom. It seemed to him that there was more than pain in her sobs. He sensed as well a comfort, a pleasure even in letting her anxiety escape so candidly. Sometimes Judith left the apartment without saying where she was going and didn't come back until evening, pale, exhausted, wild-eyed. It was pointless for Antoine to ask her where she'd been, for him to explain to her that he'd been worried. She would get undressed without listening to him and take refuge in the bed, pulling the covers over her face.

She was sometimes well-intentioned towards Antoine—she would stroke his neck when he was reading the papers, bring him a tisane, offer to run a bath—and at other times totally indifferent, spending hours shut away in the bathroom, answering his questions with inaudible murmurs. Now and then she would hover around him, trying to get his attention and then, as soon as he tried to embrace her, she would free herself violently, fling herself into an easy chair and stay there, overcome, her head in her hands, until he went away.

Antoine was afraid. He feared that Judith's stay in Paris had given her a glimpse of what a normal life could be like and that she was now trying to find a way to free herself from him. All those sighs, those silences, those bursts of affection were her way of telling him that she couldn't take any more, she couldn't help it but she had to go. He was already searching for the words to keep her there. "I need you . . . after everything we've been through together . . . We'll make it, you'll see." But all those words sounded hollow to him, and even if he could have found the language to get through to her, Antoine knew that when the time came he would be unable to speak. Perhaps Judith had quite simply met someone? The thought had often crossed his mind, but he dared not dwell on it—he needed so badly to love Judith and if that really had happened, he preferred to keep up the illusion till the end.

Now and then, especially at night, Judith would seem calmer, as if she'd stopped dreaming of an ordinary life and had accepted one made up of fear and silence. She had found new pleasures. One was making bread. Antoine would sit at the table and watch her knead the dough, her precise and solemn movements, as if she were fulfilling some grave duty on which her very life depended. Antoine liked to watch her long thin fingers plunge into the bag of flour and sprinkle some on the counter, then slowly sink into the dough and tear it into pieces before flattening it again. But at the same time her actions frightened him a little; he found as much cruelty in them as gentleness, as if some secret tie had joined that inert mass to his own body.

It was on one of those nights that Judith decided to talk. Her hoarse voice, worn out by silence, sounded to him like a stranger's.

"The night I came back from Paris I saw someone leaving your house."

Antoine was preparing to reply, to defend himself—let me explain, nothing happened, really—but Judith didn't give him time.

"I'd just parked. I saw her come down the steps and open the gate."

"Did she see you?"

"No . . . not at first."

Judith was now shaping the dough into a round ball. From where he was sitting, Antoine could see only the nape of her neck and the bottom of her right cheek. From the tone of her voice, though, he could imagine the hardness of her face. He imagined Judith concentrating on her task, determined to see it through to the end. She went on.

"I started the car again and followed her. Just as she was crossing the street, I sped up."

"Did you run over her?" asked Antoine in a muffled voice.

"I watched her in the rear-view mirror for a few moments. She was lying on the road, still. Then I drove away."

Judith finally turned towards Antoine. He was looking down, a glimmer of dread on his face.

"Who was it?" Judith asked.

"Nathalie."

"That's what I thought."

*

Paris, 11 December 2002

I hesitated for several days before I told Antoine what had happened that night. I dreaded his reaction. I was afraid of the fear on his face, as well as the horror and disgust. "You're absolutely crazy! Out of your mind! Please, tell me it's not true! You're trying to put one over on me. Say it's a bad joke, you made it up to see if I could cope, to see if I really love you..." That's what I would have liked him to say. I would have liked him to scream, to hit me, threaten to leave me—at least I'd have sensed that he was still with me. What I dreaded most was silence.

I could have kept quiet. But I'm not very good at keeping secrets. Antoine had realized as soon as I came back that something was wrong. Without wanting to, I must have scattered some clues. Eventually he was bound to understand. It was on account of him, through him, that I'd done what I had done.

When I saw that woman leaving Antoine's place I felt full of hatred. I can still see myself stepping on the gas with all my might, as if I were hurling myself into a chasm. I had no thoughts, no words in my head. At the same time though, I was entirely present, as if all the scattered parts of myself had suddenly come together, as if I were reliving a familiar scene, frozen long since in my memory. That elegant woman who was nervously crossing the street was to me merely a shadow, a semi-dream, an old recollection. That night I hadn't come to any decision. I simply agreed, without resisting, that the future would now be without hope and without respite.

*

Their life had resumed its monotonous course in the grip of fear. Fear too settles into its habits, melts into the murmur of everyday life. We don't tame it, we don't dominate it either, but eventually it becomes invisible. It interferes with every one of our thoughts, it permeates every move we make, suspends them in the expectation of a premature outcome. Antoine and Judith had become like little birds that are easily frightened, whose every beat of the wings, every peck, betrays a foreboding of danger, of the imminence of the end. They'd forgotten what a life without fear could be like. They no longer even dreamed of being carefree. They thought only about conquering every moment, about holding on for one more night, one more day.

Antoine's first reaction had been fear, not for Judith but for himself. The police would certainly conduct an investigation. Their first questions would be, "What was she doing in that part of town? Whom had she come to see?" In the end they would establish a connection between Nathalie and him; it was inevitable. He would once again be entitled to a visit from some inspectors, and this time they wouldn't let him off so easily. Associated with the deaths of two people in the space of a few months, he would surely be their prime suspect.

Antoine could have been angry with Judith. But he sensed that she was becoming more and more fragile. She now seemed like a stranger, more inscrutable than ever. He feared her reactions and, without really wanting to admit it to himself, he worried that it sometimes seemed as if she was going to lay the blame on him. When Judith's eyes rested on him, Antoine could detect, behind the exhaustion and the melancholy, the beginning of hatred.

To leave her—surely the idea had crossed his mind. But Antoine couldn't imagine living alone now; and who but Judith could put up with the secretive, stifling life in which he'd locked himself away? There was something else: oddly enough, fear had brought them closer. Under its influence Judith had become, in Antoine's eyes, at once immense and minute. Sometimes she struck him as infinitely vulnerable. She would wake up screaming in the middle of the night, or come back from a walk in a state of panic, positive she'd been followed, and Antoine would do his best to reassure her, comfort her. And sometimes, on the contrary, Judith would seem to him monstrous, not only because of what she had done but because, as far as he knew, he himself was the only witness. Their secret made her more terrifying, and the more she frightened him, the more he desired her.

*

Antoine still called Séverine now and then. He had practically nothing to say to her. He no longer tried to confide in her, but talking to her was important, even if it was just so he could go on thinking that another life would have been possible. During their most recent conversations, Séverine had seemed worried and aloof. Was one of her children sick? Was she going through a rough patch with Patrick? Just a few months ago, Antoine would have asked her, would have listened and comforted her as best he could. Without taking advantage of her vulnerability he would have found a role for himself. He would have been the one Séverine could count on, the one who lavished advice, who was always there. But Antoine could no longer read Séverine's mind. He was aware of her concern, but he couldn't reach her. And in the gulf that was gradually opening between them he saw the gaping hole that separated him henceforth from ordinary life.

*

Paris, 13 December 2002

For some time now I've been sleeping very badly. All is well until two or three in the morning, but then it's over. Impossible to get back to sleep despite my exhaustion. I think about Antoine. I would like him to be close to me, but it's not really him that I want. It's his body that I miss, his physical presence, the feel of his skin. He is now merely a void that I can't fill, a need to touch, to be held, that follow me wherever I go.

I think constantly about what happened. Even though I know that trying to understand is futile, I keep turning over the events in my head, I keep looking for the trigger, the one moment that started everything. But I'm not tormented by the thought that it could all have been avoided. The truth is that we no longer knew how to love one another. We had thought that we could mend time, wipe out the past, begin again as if we'd just found one another. In fact, though, we were filled with hatred and spite—particularly me—and the only desire that remained was made up of violence and despair. Perhaps remorse will come, who knows? And when it comes I will know that it's time to leave.

Paris, 14 December 2002

I had the same dream last night. I'm lying on my back, stark naked. Between my legs something is tickling me. At first I think it's a thread of eiderdown but I realize when I pull on it that it's coming from my body. I feel it rub against the walls of my sex. It's a whitish thread, slightly sticky, that appears to be coated with wax or glue. I wonder how it got there. Maybe it's not a thread, maybe it's some kind of worm that has settled inside my body and grown in my entrails unbeknownst to me, for months and months. I keep pulling. The thread gets a little thicker. Now its texture is rubbery, like a soft, gooey tentacle. Panicking, I pull faster and faster and still there is that unpleasant sensation between my legs, that cold, vibrant thing escaping from my sex. I tell myself that it will soon be over, that this thing will eventually leave and then one day I'll be able to get up, set free. But I keep pulling and the oily cord, thicker and thicker, glides and wriggles like an eel between my tense fingers. It's as if my guts are being emptied, unravelled, dragged out of me, but when I look, terrified, at the long cord of flesh that is accumulating at my feet, I don't feel transformed; inside my body, nothing has changed. The thing emerges, unendingly unwinds, as if it were coming not from my body but from the entrails of the earth. And soon I don't even need to pull. It flows out of me like a snake emerging from its shelter. It runs away. I can't hold it in; it spews itself out uncontrollably. I'm afraid and at the same time I'm impatient. Impatient for nothing to remain, for only my carcass to be left, so that I can at last find rest and close my eyes.

Even when I wake up, exhausted, the dream hasn't altogether stopped. The sensation is still there, of that cold mass that slides between my legs, that runs away, that I cannot hold back.

*

They left around the end of June. They'd often talked about leaving London, but always very vaguely, never making concrete plans. If Antoine had been asked how they'd decided to leave and why they'd chosen the south of France, he wouldn't have been able to say. One night Judith had come in, saying, "Why don't we go away?" Antoine hadn't reacted at once, but after a few moments, he'd put down his newspaper, followed

Judith into the bedroom and taken two suitcases out of the closet. The next morning they were on their way to Dover.

In the car, with her nose in an old map of France, Judith felt strangely free, as she had on the day when she'd left by herself for Paris. On the boat later, they walked back and forth holding hands. They didn't look at each other, but they were smiling. And in the eyes of people they met, they were certainly no different from any other young couple who'd taken off for a long weekend and were quietly savouring their first moments of freedom.

For the first time in months, Antoine felt somewhat calm. His mind was busy now with practical questions to which he could easily find the answers. "Where shall we stop for the night? Where should we go for breakfast? Shall we spend a few days in Lyon?" Every time, he consulted Judith and gradually, their inconsequential conversations restored some normality to their lives.

They spent a few days in Nice. In the morning they would sit on a café terrace. Antoine read the papers while Judith watched the passing crowd. Fear hadn't loosened its grip, but under the June sky, in a city they'd discovered together and where they didn't know a soul, it had another texture, another rhythm. It didn't assail them first thing after they woke up; it developed slowly, a little at a time, as the charm of the new day dwindled. In the afternoon, after a good lunch, which they would draw out until three o'clock, the first signs of anxiety, without contours or content, began to disturb their carefree attitude. They continued their walk in the city, but their hearts weren't in it. Passersby struck them as sad and lifeless, the heat weighed heavily on them, the idleness they savoured so fully in the morning now made them feverish, and as their minds could find no future point to settle on, they went back inevitably to the past and to the certainty that they were only experiencing a moment of reprieve. They dined lightly, hastily, in a small bistro across from the hotel. Back in their room they watched television and waited for sleep to come. When they finally nodded off, it was from exhaustion and without pleasure.

After a few days they got back on the road. They went first to Antibes, then turned around and went back, criss-crossing the coast: Juan-les-Pins, Cannes, Grasse, Monaco, Menton. They went from hotel to hotel, never spending more than two nights in the same place. The peaceful beauty of the landscapes, the appeal of the old parts of town, the new aromas of the hinterland—they were indifferent to it all. They no longer hoped to regain peace, calm, the certainty of distant hopes. They were only looking for the moment of respite that accompanies departures, when one is receptive, when the unexpected is possible again and one expects nothing. By moving from town to town, from village to village, they had the impression that they were losing themselves, disconnecting themselves from a sense of place, becoming merely characters without a soul to whom nothing mattered, able to do everything and to whom everything could happen. It was existence without the immense wall against which their future was being shattered.

*

They spent a day at Monte Carlo. They browsed in the shops, visited the aquarium and went at night to the casino. For Antoine as for Judith, it was a new and mythical world that they knew only from movies. To them the sinister-looking croupier, the elegant women in low-cut gowns, the fleshy men with lecherous eyes could have come straight out of an American film from the 1950s. They felt out of place, but the haughty gazes of the regulars didn't intimidate them. They got some chips and bravely approached a table where roulette was being played. They waited for a player to leave—a young man with a sad expression who'd just won a large sum—and sat across from the croupier. Judith took the time to observe the action around the table for a few minutes. Red, black, red, black: the little ball moved regularly from one colour to the other. When the black came up, Judith would bet on red—and when it was the turn of red she'd bet on black. She played again the chip she'd just won on black—and won again. Then on red, again on black, and every time more chips were added to her winnings. Totally possessed by gambling, Judith should have felt a rising excitement in her body, she should have forgotten the world around her and thought herself invincible. On the contrary, however, she seemed perfectly calm, and even when she began to lose, she was serene, like someone who doesn't gamble for the money or who has set out secretly to sabotage her own game. Now and then she looked up in the direction of the other players. They would give her sidelong glances, having realized that this was a novice. Feigning indifference, they waited eagerly for her to snap. Judith, though, remained impassive. She wasn't like them. Her life, her future did not depend on the money she would win or lose that night. Nothing that happened to her could touch her now. She no longer experienced, as the other players did, the desire for power and self-loathing. She had even lost the despair that could have spurred her on, that could have made her hope for a different life.

*

Paris, 18 December 2002

When did we talk about death for the first time? Sudden death. Not to see the death of the other, not to feel the end approaching. Force ourselves to believe that we would not be separated, not because we'd run away together but because we'd had the same desire, the same courage.

*

With the money Judith had put aside after the gallery was sold they rented a villa in the vicinity of Nice. Situated at the top of a hill, it was surrounded by trees, and a small corner of the sea was visible from the bedroom. The last occupants had left all sorts of traces: cigarette butts, unwashed glasses and plates, old newspapers. A few months earlier Judith would have thrown herself into a massive housecleaning and persuaded Antoine to give her a hand. But they were no longer concerned about their comfort. They no longer cared about sleeping in clean sheets or wearing pressed clothes.

Antoine woke up early in the morning to go for a swim in the garden pool. Sometimes Judith would watch him from the bedroom window; his slender body slashed the water like an arrow, slowly, systematically; his precise, methodical motions were reminiscent of a machine that goes on turning, inexorably, even if it is no longer of any use. He swam like that till he was exhausted; draining away all his energy also drained away his fear.

Afternoons they went to Nice to do their shopping. To avoid having to use the car—whose British licence plate was liable to attract attention—Antoine had bought a used Vespa. Judith got on behind him, wrapped her arms around his waist and rested her head on his back. Those brief moments were for her a flicker of respite. She closed her eyes and let herself be carried away, the freshness of the wind, Antoine's hair tickling her face. Secretly she wished for death. She dreamed of an accident: Antoine driving off the road at the edge of a precipice. They would fall together, a few seconds of total freedom that would seal their lives, a few seconds they could perhaps surreptitiously carry away in their memory.

Sometimes they had lunch in Nice. They avoided crowds and preferred to take refuge in a park, safe from tourists and vacationers. They watched children playing on swings, energy intact, free of fear, devoted entirely to the moment. The mothers talked among themselves, now and then breaking off their conversation to give some advice to their child or to ward off a disaster: "Don't take off your sandals, sweetheart, you might get cut!" "Don't swing too high, remember how you got hurt last time!" In the way they moved, in their candid, healthy smiles, their lightheartedness was so natural that it gave the impression that they deserved their happiness. Judith didn't envy them, but their display of ordinary joy broke her heart. She realized that her life was now closed off, that no happiness, not even the most simple, was within her reach.

Back at the villa that evening, they felt as if they were nowhere, as if they'd already started to leave the world a little. Antoine sat on the terrace and did crosswords while Judith read old whodunits she'd found in the bedroom closet. But immobility created anxiety, and they felt a constant need to move on, to change location, to leave behind them the places that had briefly brought them back to themselves. When they grew restless they got on the Vespa and went back to Nice. There they wandered from bar to bar, from hotel to hotel.

They would come home in the middle of the night, exhausted and drunk. It was not till later, when they woke up long after sunrise, that they would embrace and seek pleasure together, putting off the moment when their everyday terror would take hold of them again.

*

"This can't go on."

"No."

"They'll end up ... They'll come here, that's for sure."

"Yes."

"And then, it'll all be over."

"Yes. Unless we die first."

Antoine looks up at Judith. He's been expecting her to be crushed, her face to be dark and expressionless. But she looks at him defiantly, with the beginning of a smile at the corners of her lips, like a child who's not afraid to admit that she's just done something extremely stupid.

"What do you mean, Judith?"

"We just have to ... I don't know, we could jump off a cliff together. Don't you think that would be a good way to die?"

"I'm serious, Judith, I don't know how much longer I can hang on."

"I'm serious too, I think about it all the time. Sooner or later we'll have to make up our minds. I can't see any other solution."

*

They touch, they kiss only when they make love. And even then, they only seek the efficiency of pleasure. They avoid looking one another in the eyes and let themselves be absorbed entirely by their hands, which, like industrious spiders, travel slowly along their bodies' furrows. And in the shudder of that contact, their entire beings rush back to the surface, erasing along the way all the questions, all the anxieties that bruise their everyday lives. Their sole concern then is to make the moment last, because they know that as soon as they come, their fear will return.

*

Paris, 23 December 2002

We were talking more and more about death—Antoine had gotten a revolver and we were constructing a number of scenarios in which we would die together and without suffering. Those thoughts were comforting. The fear was still there but we could silence it any time, which made us feel as if we were able to overcome it. We could play with fear, let it grow inside us, interfere with our modest pleasures, stimulate our desire and then, when it suffocated us, when it threatened to swamp us, we just had to think about death and in one fell swoop we were free. All was lost, but at least we could choose the ending. In our frenzy of terror we would tell each other that perhaps we would experience again a fragment of the complete moment that had once revealed us to one another, and that we had since tried in vain to recover.

*

Nice, 15 August 2002

> Dear Séverine,
> *For some time now I have been a different man. My life has taken a turn with consequences I have not yet been able to grasp. I'm caught in a spiral from which I cannot escape. It has become my whole life. I no longer belong to myself. I see no way out.*
>
> *I hesitated for a long time before writing you. I was afraid of imposing a confession on you that would unsettle you more than I could imagine, one that would totally transform your opinion of me. At the same time though you are the only*

one to whom I can open up completely, and I've come to the conclusion that you more than anyone else are entitled to know what has happened in my life.

Here it is then: it all started last October. Judith and I had gone to a pub in Chelsea for a drink. By a most unfortunate stroke of bad luck, we ran into a former colleague of mine—the one with whom I'd been unfaithful to Judith nine years ago . . .

Antoine knows he won't finish the letter. He doesn't have the strength. He knew that even before he started. Sitting in the bathroom, he asks himself: "Why bother? These are just the facts. And facts don't explain anything. What really matters I could never give voice to. Séverine would have to understand—she who is so rational and reasonable—that Judith and I never agreed to squander our love, that we have let jealousy gnaw at us, that our past, our memories have never left us, that they constantly rush back, that they don't give us a moment's respite. We dream, absurdly, of going back in time, of wiping out the past, of returning, intact, to the first time we met. And now that we've come to this, now that we have nothing left to lose, God knows what we're still capable of doing."

*

> "The body of Virginie Rivière was discovered on a beach in Nice yesterday afternoon. Police assume the death was due to drowning, but scratches on the arms and shoulders raise the possibility that the young woman was the victim of an attack."

When he reads about Virginie's death in the *Quotidien de Nice*, Antoine is floored. There's no doubt about it, it is Virginie; after they separated, he remembers, Virginie had left Paris and moved down to the Côte d'Azur.

At once, a new fear settles into him: there was Kate, then Nathalie and now Virginie. The police are bound to track him down; it's inevitable. The investigators will discover that he knew all three women—and what's more, that he had been their lover—and they'll draw their own conclusions. Even if he had no part in the deaths of Nathalie and Virginie, before long his name will be added to the list of suspects. He'll have to undergo another interrogation and this time he's not sure that he'll be able to deal with it. He will betray himself, he may betray Judith, and instead of realizing their dream of dying together, they'll both end up in prison, two pathetic lovers blinded by rage and violence.

Sitting on the terrace and looking up at the sky, Antoine is contemplating the eucalyptus whose smooth, silky branches wrap him in shadows, like an affectionate gesture. But he senses that from now on there will be neither peace nor comfort; they will spend the rest of their lives lying low and running away like hunted animals. Antoine rereads the article.

"Scratches on the arms and shoulders raise the possibility that the young woman was the victim of an attack." An absurd suspicion crosses his mind; he represses it at once. It's not possible. She'd never be able to do that. And yet certain circumstances would seem to justify his doubts. Lately Judith has been getting up very early, taking the scooter and going for a ride along the sea. When he asked her about her absences, Judith had explained that she had more and more trouble sleeping and that the fresh air was good for her. Then, when he woke up yesterday, he had found Judith curled up on the grass near the pool. Her hair was wet, her fists clenched on her chest. She was crying silently. When Antoine approached her she didn't react. There was a faraway look in her eyes and tears were running down her still face, like raindrops on waxen cheeks.

Later, he'd gone into the bathroom while Judith was taking her shower. He had noticed bruises on her arms and scrapes on her neck and back. She claimed that she'd fallen on her way down the stairs to the villa. She'd thought she was being followed and, panicking, she had stumbled and fallen into the undergrowth. Antoine found her story hard to believe, but he didn't understand why she would have lied to him, so he'd let the matter drop. He only helped her to lie down, wiped her forehead with cold water and put peroxide on her scrapes. Now the day's events were taking on an altogether different meaning. What if her story about a fall was a lie? And what if Judith had followed Virginie that day? And what if—and what if she was the one?

She would have had to know that Virginie lived nearby. What if she'd seen Virginie's family name in an old address book? Knowing that Virginie was a journalist, Judith would then have searched the Net and learned that she was a correspondent for the *Quotidien de Nice*. All plausible, but then what? Judith would have had to find out where she lived, follow her, track her comings and goings. How else could she know that Virginie was going to be at the seaside at that time precisely? One morning, then, she would have hidden behind a rock not far from the place where Virginie was in the habit of going to swim. She would have waited for her to go in the water, let her swim out a little, then she too would have slipped into the waves. She'd have swum after Virginie and, once she was close to her, attacked her by surprise...

Antoine gets up. Hands stuffed in the pockets of his shorts, head down, he paces the garden. He feels dazed, the world starts to sway around him, he has to sit down. He looks towards the bedroom window. Judith is still asleep. He imagines her hugging her pillow, like a child with her teddy bear, her face at peace under the soft sun that enters through the partly open shutters. No, she couldn't have done it. Those morning walks along the seashore, those scrapes and bruises— they could be sheer coincidence. And didn't the article mention that Virginie was investigating drug rings in the area? After all, it was entirely possible that she'd been eliminated to silence her.

*

Antoine won't speak to Judith about Virginie's death. From now on what they share is silence. Beyond the confidence that words provide, they are pulled in one another's direction, two wandering creatures converging towards the certainty of death. The time for questions is past. Weigh, assess, hesitate: Antoine is no longer doing any of that. Is doubt not an admission that his life can still follow another course, that his will belongs to him even now? When he looks inside himself, when he stops justifying his decisions or trying to find a logic for his acts, Antoine realizes that he knows everything he needs to know about Judith. This is not a truth that he can express clearly; rather it's something like a hunch that keeps growing inside him, that sweeps through and paralyzes him: the certainty that Judith and he will never again be separated, that all his actions are merely shadows of hers and that lodged in every one of Judith's desires is his own resolution, complete, urgent and blind.

*

Antoine is lying on the grass by the pool, lulled by the chirping of crickets. Though the sun burns his eyelids, he doesn't move. He listens to the sound of the water, the monotonous back and forth of Judith swimming lengths. He follows her movements: curling herself into a ball, doing a somersault underwater, then raising her head for a moment before going on. From the sound her arms make he guesses that she's swimming on her back, then she moves on to a crawl and finally to a breaststroke. Her hands, quick and nimble, appear to stroke the surface of the water. Judith swims, he thinks, as if she were walking on tiptoe, as if she were afraid of waking some malevolent creature lurking at the bottom of the pool.

In the midday sun, Antoine doesn't have the strength to move. The intense heat bathes his face and enters his lungs. He has trouble breathing. Big drops of sweat stand out on his forehead like blisters on an invalid's skin. Now and then one of them runs down his temple and into the corner of his eye, stinging. Antoine should get up, he should go and sit in the shade, but his body no longer obeys him. He feels lighter and lighter, as if he's being lifted by the blinding light. It's a strange sensation: he is paralyzed, but at the same time he feels as if he is floating. He feels carried away as well by the murmur of the water, that shimmering music that pierces like a blade of light through the glum song of the crickets. A sudden coolness spreads through him. He is back with Judith—or rather, no, his body has gradually merged with hers. Now it's his own fingers that graze effortlessly the surface of the water, his legs that propel him forward.

And now the water caressing his face tastes of salt. He is no longer in the pool but in the sea. The being he has become, the Antoine-Judith, is tossed about by the waves. He swims towards the horizon, unconcerned that he can no longer see the shore. The sun still blinds him, but it is a fluid heat that hugs his body and carries it out to sea. After a few minutes he spots something that resembles a buoy. He swims up to it and realizes that it's actually a woman's head, her long hair a dark streak behind her. Now Antoine wants to go back to shore, but he feels irresistibly drawn to the woman. Driven by a strange force, he no longer belongs to himself. He is now only a body—his own? Judith's?—that is getting closer to the swimmer. In a few moments he will have caught up with her. And then, taking advantage of the surprise, he will throw himself onto her, push her head under the water, hold onto her arms, which will struggle furiously, resist the punches, ignore the desperate cries and finally bear down on the woman's shoulders with his full weight until she disappears under the waves.

Exhausted, Antoine allows himself to drift. He feels numb and disoriented, as if he were emerging from a lengthy torpor. Is the sea carrying his inert body or is the light wrapping him in warmth and silence? He finally opens his eyes, raises his head awkwardly and realizes that Judith is no longer in the pool. He gets up and staggers to the villa. Sitting at the kitchen table, Judith is eating a slice of bread with Nutella. She seems not to have noticed him. When he sits down beside her she puts her hand on his and smiles at him. Her dry lips have a painful and tender expression. In her gaze though there is no emotion. Her eyes that in the past said so much to Antoine now hide nothing, reveal no secret; and into their void Antoine is slowly sinking, he too given over to hatred, overcome by a fierce desire to see it through to the bitter end.

*

Paris, 28 December 2002

Did he want that storm of violence the way I wanted it, or did he simply let himself be carried away because he knew that he couldn't stop me? Where did I find the courage, the determination to go so far? Even today, with the advantage of distance, I'm not sure I understand. I was obsessed by a desire to regain the feelings I'd had for Antoine when we first met. It was the pursuit of that chimera that made me so unhappy and that prevented us, I now realize, from enjoying what we had. In the frenzy that was gradually sweeping me away, I told myself that if we hadn't been able to go back to the way we'd been, it was because we'd been sullied by the memories of all those who had crossed our lives, who had kept us estranged from each other.

*

Now and then Antoine thinks back to the time he and Séverine had spent together in Cannes and Antibes several years earlier. He remembers their conversations, their strolls along the Croisette, the restaurants where they had lunch. But those memories no longer belong to him. They are the memories of someone else and he has taken possession of them, furtively, like a thief who has secretly taken part of his loot to jail. Those memories are from another life, a life in which the future was a white desert and where promises had the perfection of dreams.

*

Antoine looks at Judith. Naked, dozing on the sofa, one last ray of sunlight extinguished on her face, she seems to him so vulnerable, so delicate. She's not beautiful. Not to others at any rate. Her angular hips, her knobby knees, the veins that run along her thin arms, her protruding ribs—there's not enough flesh on her body to kindle desire. His eyes light on her breasts, which are hardly breasts at all. Barely small swellings, as if they'd just appeared, as if, exposed to the light and people's eyes, they were about to vanish again. Moved, Antoine approaches her, holds out his hand to touch her, imagining already the cool dampness of her skin under his fingers, then decides not to. He feels as if he's doing something forbidden. Judith, naked in front of him, is another woman, an unknown woman, a stranger; or maybe his alter ego, his newly found dream, his sister.

In a few moments Judith will wake up. She may be a little surprised to see Antoine standing in front of her, but won't let it show. She will ask him how long he's been there, whether she talked in her sleep—or rather, no, she'll simply smile at him and take him with her to the bedroom. There, both of them kneeling on the floor, they will pretend to discover one another. Antoine will close his eyes so he can't see Judith's hands. He won't be able to stop thinking about what they have done, about what they could still do. When he opens his eyes there will be in Judith's gaze a new brightness, a certainty, a determination that he'd never known. He'll think to himself, "She had eyes that knew how to laugh." He will no longer tolerate being looked at by her, facing that countenance which now will only tell the story of how it ended.

When he finally enters her, the pleasure will come not from their bodies but from the awareness, now immense and clear, of what they have achieved, of the unspeakable actions of which they are capable, of their senseless courage and of their own death, which is now drawing near.

*

A few days later Antoine comes back from grocery shopping to find Judith busy packing their bags.

Quickly opening all the drawers, she flings their clothes every which way onto the bed. Noticing Antoine in the doorway looking bewildered, she stops for a moment. Calmly, she says to him, "Give me a hand. We're leaving."

"What's going on, Judith?"

"Two policemen were just here."

"What did they want?"

Antoine's voice is nothing but a murmur. He has dreaded this moment. He feels as if he's in the cast of a play that Judith and he have spent a long time rehearsing.

"No idea. They wanted to talk to you."

"How do they know ... What did you tell them?"

"Nothing. That you weren't here, you'd gone to Marseille for a few days."

"They believed you?"

"I have no idea. Probably not. Anyway, it doesn't matter. We have to go, that's all."

Antoine feels completely broken. Faced with a thousand questions that plague him, his mind is powerless, going feverishly from one to another without managing to resolve a single one. Have the French police been informed by their British colleagues? How did they know that he was in Nice? Do they want to question him about the death of Virginie? Do they know what connected him to Judith? Even if he manages to shed light on those questions, he'll be no further ahead. The noose is tightening; it's all that matters now. At this point their only choice is to run away. It's the one freedom still available to them and with that certainty, Antoine is trying, against all hope, to find one last source of comfort.

That evening they set out for Paris.

*

Paris, 8 January 2003

We left a few days later. Didn't even bother to sell the Vespa or pack all our belongings.

In the car we talked feverishly about death. About death from a bullet, from jumping off a bridge, from hanging, poisoning; we weighed the pros and cons. And the more we talked about it, the more death seemed to us logical, necessary. But it wasn't simply the desire to be done with it. We also felt that we were finally close to one another. In the vacuum we'd created around us there was nothing but that strange thing, that immense thing we were going to accomplish. We were coming home after wandering for a long time and we were about to cross the threshold. At the edge of the abyss we were going to relive, in a dark light, like a photo negative, the enchantment of the first moments. Everything we did, everything we said to one another, would have the same weight as the first time, because it would be the last. Every touch would be the invention of touch, every smile the invention of smiling, because they would never be repeated, they would be crystallized in the light of the end.

That's all insane, I now realize, but neither Antoine nor I was in any state to argue. Knowing that in a few days we would vanish had made us suddenly feel weightless. There were no more obstacles. We could do anything, think anything. We had convinced ourselves that nothing could stop us now, that because it was pulling us along towards the end, our will was stronger than the life we were leaving behind. We were ending our existence as masters because neither death nor our fellow humans had a hold over us any longer.

We felt exalted and at the same time terrified. I don't remember whether Antoine and I really talked about all that or whether those thoughts, created by my awareness exclusively, were so real in my eyes that it seemed to me inconceivable that Antoine didn't have them in him as well. We finally had a shared goal, a project that no one could take away from us. As we drew closer we felt ourselves growing, transformed into imaginary, extraordinary beings. We were now just a single will and even if we weren't sure that we possessed it entirely, it gave us confidence because it allowed us to think that the two of us were now just a single life.

In a small hotel room in Lyon, I watched Antoine sleep. He seemed peaceful, exhausted after driving for several hours. I thought I could make out the beginning of a smile and that smile seemed to me to be all that was left of him. Antoine was already dead; he was only a memory, weighing more and more, that I carried inside me, that I was taking towards death. And I myself was beginning to dissolve. I was his dream that he didn't want to give back to the world, that he was trying to protect against life.

*

It is a thought that comes to him without a word, without an image. It is merely a shadow in his mind, like the premonition that one is being watched, but not knowing why or by whom. Judith in his arms strikes him as immense, as infinitely powerful. Those hands that touch his nape, that move down his back, can decide about death. He tightens his embrace, buries his face in her neck, as if she is about to dissolve. She is no longer the one his body imagines; she is a thousand other women who know nothing about him. They all escape, indifferent to him, each one towards her own end.

He would like to say, "I'm afraid of you." But that wouldn't be altogether true. He would have to be able to say at the same time, "I wish I were you."

She takes hold of his sex, guides it into her. She tells him to bite her, to bite her neck, her shoulders. Usually he stops as soon as she pushes him away. This time though she lets him go on, doesn't say a word even if the pain is unbearable. His teeth sink a little more deeply into her flesh; at any moment he expects to hear her say, "Stop, please stop," but she remains impassive as if, already, her body no longer belongs to her. When he finally lets go she looks at him, dark and impassive. But her legs are slightly parted. He feels her squeezing him, his sex burns as it's drawn a little deeper inside her. He imagines the wave of pleasure spreading through her, along her thighs, moving along her hips, her arms, then dying in the hollow of her shoulders. When he opens his eyes, Judith's face hasn't changed: neither pain nor peace nor relief. Nothing, perhaps, but the eager contemplation of the final moment.

His earlier thought begins then to take shape, another shape, perhaps: it's no longer Judith but a body to which he's just made love, a still-warm mass of life from which consciousness has been removed. Judith is already far away and her body is no longer there except to guide him, to help him also to desert the world.

*

Paris, 10 January 2003

I was delirious, and I took Antoine along in my delirium. But it was filled with reasons, with resolutions and promises and plans. I explained to Antoine that he must find my other lovers, those I'd known during our separation. I described for him what to do, how to go about it. I would give him the addresses, I would tell him everything I knew about them, about their lives. He would follow them, learn their habits, their routine, the places they went, and when the time came... At first I didn't actually realize what I was saying. I let myself be carried away by the abstract, crazy image that had gradually taken shape in me, the image of a pure love, an intimacy that we would get back by immolating our past. Then, gradually, I started to believe it.

I told Antoine that all the years we'd spent apart had been an anomaly; we should never have been separated. I told him, all that is left is to burn up our memories, to abolish time. When they are dead nothing will come between us, I'd be his entirely. He listened to me, impassive. Maybe he was afraid, maybe he'd have liked to give up everything, but we had already gone so far together, he couldn't have opposed me. Once we had set off along that road, we wouldn't have been able to go back. We were free in the way that only death can set one free.

Nothing mattered to us anymore. By choosing to die we had opened in time a space for freedom where nothing more could reach us, where everything was allowed. Death had spread death all around us; it had swallowed up all the perspectives. The time that remained was blank now, gradually purged of our story, of our cowardice, our compromises. All that lay ahead of us was the abyss, vast and untouched, where all the possibilities were calling us.

I said to Antoine, during the time before our death our deeds are weightless—the world ceases to exist before we do. Every one of our deeds, once accomplished, is already fading, as if tinted by the shadow of our imminent death. That chunk of time, withdrawn from the world, is like the light that comes to us from a long-dead star—a parenthesis of nothingness before the absence of consciousness.

Our deeds, our desires, our dreams all have the same consistency. Killing a man, a dog or a flower amounts to the same thing. We're free because we are already dead. We are free because by choosing death we have pierced a hole in time.

5

Paris, 12 January 2003

Once we were back in Paris, we started to look for Alain. I knew where he worked, in what neighbourhood he lived, and it wasn't too hard to track him down. Antoine started to keep an eye on his comings and goings and at night he gave me a report of what he'd observed. Our discussions were logistic in nature. It was simply a question of finding the best way—so that the end of Alain would be decisive and painless and that Antoine wouldn't be arrested. He reasoned calmly, his voice steady, preoccupied only with the effectiveness of his actions, like an architect reviewing the day's work on a construction site.

At times though he woke up in the middle of the night, gasping for breath, soaked in sweat. He no longer told me his nightmares, but when he turned towards me I could make out in his empty gaze—devoid of emotion, of will, even of fear—the gulf into which he'd descended. He rested his head on my chest and I stroked his hair, half-hoping that he would share his dreams. But he treated his anxiety as a physical obstacle he had to surmount. When he had exhausted the possibilities of alcohol or sleep, he would come closer to my body. What was awakened then was no longer desire but the reflexes that go along with desire: the shudder that runs up the back, the dilated pupils, the lips engorged with blood, the faster breathing. In the blankness of his gaze as he contemplated my body there was no tenderness now, no compassion: only the frenzy of a hunted animal tearing off one last chunk of life before it finally succumbs. I realize now that I was no longer the woman he loved but the one who could kill, the one he must follow, the scarcely alive reflection of his own disappearance. He wanted me with all the life still in him because I was now the outcome, the only end for which he was allowed to hope.

*

Antoine looks at the man who is standing on the deserted platform. He is reading his paper. He is thinking about what he'll do once he gets back home; he thinks about his wife who is watching the news, lying in bed, waiting for his return; he may also be thinking about tomorrow, about the report he has to finish.

Every evening on his way home from work, standing on the platform at Exelmans station, he has the same thoughts. Day by day he pushes his small life ahead of him, with its small tasks, its small plans, its small pleasures. Tonight though, it's harder. The man's daydreaming is even more vain, more fragile than usual. The man doesn't know it, but he is already dead.

For Antoine this ignorance is reassuring. He won't have to look at the fear on the man's face. When the time comes he will just have to push him—a few steps, a simple movement of the arms, then he'll turn his head. No one will have seen a thing: the man won't have seen death and Antoine won't have seen him die.

Antoine knows hardly anything about this man. His name is Alain, he met Judith, she thought she loved him, then he left. They may have without realizing it dreamed of a future when they would be together, when they too would mimic the gestures of love. But none of that matters now.

Antoine is no longer afraid. It's not that he has overcome fear. It's still there, but transformed. Fear is now his desperate resolve, the great empty space that has settled into him, his love for Judith, his desire to be done with it. His actions have no more weight than dreams do because he too has already started to die. And for the man he is now approaching he feels neither hatred nor contempt. In truth, knowing what the man does not know—will know only at the moment when everything disappears—brings him closer: Antoine sees himself standing on the platform. It is him, Antoine, who is reading his paper, thinking about his wife, about his dinner, about his bed; it is him who is thinking about tomorrow, who hears the rumble of the approaching train; it is him who doesn't know it, but who is already dead.

*

Paris, 15 January 2003

After Alain's death things become confused in my memory. I probably started talking to Antoine about Laurent—without naming him perhaps. Most likely I told him that we should finish what we'd started, that soon, very soon, we would finally have burned our entire past, we would belong fully to one another. Was he able to detect in my elation, in my confusion, a kind of reluctance? Did he, without saying so, feel that my passionate declarations might in fact be the early stage of doubt?

We still talked sometimes about our first meeting. Turning it over and over in our minds we had elevated it like an effigy above all our memories. But after dominating my thoughts for so long, it was beginning gradually to lose its clarity and colour. I had dreamed of it so much, meditated on it so often, as if on the threshold of my existence, that I could no longer tell the difference between what was remembered and what was invented. Those few months of careless love and light had indeed existed, but all the rest—the perfect intimacy, the impenetrable certainty about the future, the end of all questions—had I not imposed it upon my memory, had I not painted in a series of layers all the hopes, the vague desires and the consolations that had accumulated since our separation? Had I really wanted to know what those few months of happiness with Antoine had been, I would have had to leave my memories in peace. Each return creates a new misrepresentation on the surface of the past; when we come back to the same memory too often, it becomes unrecognizable in the end.

*

The icy tip of the revolver on her temple. The cold spreads slowly across her cheek, her neck, her shoulder, like a streak of frost. A shudder that resembles pleasure, Judith thinks, a final seduction, a man's breath on her skin trying for one last time to hold her back. Antoine standing beside her—his hand, which has been holding the revolver for too long, starts to tremble slightly. Judith forces herself to keep her eyes open. She looks at the white wall of the bedroom, the cracked ceiling, the old wooden desk, their clothes scattered over the bed. All the objects seem to her suddenly stamped with a unique new meaning, as if bathed in the first light of dawn. She began to name them: table, window, bed, as if she were discovering them, as if she were inventing them. But each word also opens a crack in the world. "Vase," and the vase disappears. "Cup": the cup is no longer there. "Ashtray": the ashtray's turn to be erased. TV, glass, curtains: once named, the objects disintegrate before her eyes. For each one, a new sentence is uttered, another cavity is drawn on the surface of silence. From one breach to the next, there is nothing more than a world in shreds, small, scattered pieces of existence, lightless glints of a shapeless mass.

The revolver trembles more and more. Judith dares not turn around to look at Antoine. His eyes are surely closed; he would be incapable of watching her die. She does not tell herself, "That's it, it's over." She is no longer thinking about death. She is no longer thinking about Antoine or their past. Already, he is no longer there; it's no longer him. What she senses now is merely a vague presence that is also rushing back to the invisible. Judith is now alone. Before her wide-open eyes drained of desire there is nothing but this lacerated world and behind it, the impenetrable mass of the future, purged of all possibilities.

Suddenly, a muffled sound startles her: the revolver has fallen to the ground. Antoine has collapsed onto a chair, sweating, distraught. Judith approaches him, kneels by the chair, runs her hand over his damp hair. Then buries her head in his shoulder so she won't have to meet his eyes.

*

Paris, 17 January 2003

I wish I didn't have to talk about her. I'd suspected for some time that he was still in touch with her. There had been the time in Nice when I'd caught him on the phone and he'd hung up as soon as he saw me coming. I should have realized, but I was deluded. I needed too badly to believe that we were united, that our senseless determination would eventually take us back to that lost moment when nothing mattered, when nothing existed except us.

It was when I saw them together in the deserted café that I understood. But was there really anything to understand? Everything was so confused in my mind. I tried to tell myself: no, it's not what you think, she's just a friend, you're the one he loves, it's to you that he gives himself... But I was so upset I couldn't reason. I was questioning everything. I thought: If he has to say goodbye to her, it means he's no longer with me entirely. I didn't even wonder what they were saying to each other, if he'd talked to her about us. I didn't need that to feel betrayed.

If I'd brought it up with him he'd have protested: Séverine is just a friend, there's never been anything between us, I swear. And that may be, in fact, what is most difficult for me to accept: because they hadn't slept together, because maybe they hadn't even kissed, there was something between them that could never exist between us.

Paris, 18 January 2003

It's the future that keeps us from dying. If it were only a question of dying today it wouldn't be so hard to accept. It's easy enough to give up the pleasures of one day. But when we die we must die every day, without ever coming back. From the vantage point of death, the future is always infinite, even when we have just one day left to live. Faced with nothingness, it is always a portion of eternity that we lose.

Paris, 19 January 2003

I would have liked to live my life the way we experience memories: drifting freely from one to the next, abandoning nonchalantly the ones that irritate us or depress us, repeating ad nauseam those that elevate us, those that would have saved us—if only we'd been sufficiently aware of them.

Paris, 20 January 2003

I would have liked this diary to be a refuge. I would have liked it to reflect not the person I feel in me but the one I forgot, the one I could never see and who during all that time knew who I was, studied my every move, patiently waited to be invited for a face-to-face. But all I find in it are the voice of someone else, foreign memories, life-condemning words.

Paris, 21 January 2003

I remember the warmth of his hand squeezing mine, as if he wanted that contact to assume the meaning of all the words he could no longer say. The wind was gusting and the rain was lashing our faces. I tried to convince myself that Antoine's hand in mine was all

I'd dreamed of, all I'd lived for. I repeated to myself: there is no one but me, no one but him. We've finally found one another. But those words were no longer alive. Another thought came back, rose up above all these beautiful thoughts: you are not the only one. There is the other woman; she was always there. He never stopped thinking about her. He may be thinking about her right now.

If at the very last moment I let go of his hand, if I didn't jump with him, it was not out of cowardice or fear. It was because I could no longer hear his voice, because I was no longer sure that I could guess his thoughts. The man who was standing on the Pont du Garigliano holding my hand, the man who gazed with me at the impenetrable darkness of the Seine, was no longer Antoine. He was only a memory, a shadow, an imaginary being—similar to the ones children sometimes create when they are too lonely.

When my hand let go of his he didn't try to hold on to it. He didn't even turn around.

Paris, 27 January 2003

They came yesterday afternoon. Two of them. Polite, amiable, they seemed not at all threatening. They asked some questions about Antoine, then had me follow them to the station to take my statement. How long had I known Antoine Lemercier? What was the nature of our relationship? Was I present at the moment of his death? Why had he committed suicide? Had I tried to stop him? Had he had mental-health problems in the past? And then they asked me about Alain d'Orangeville. They asked me if I knew him, if Antoine knew him. Antoine was suspected of causing his death last October 12. Was I with him that night?

After two hours they let me go. I went back to the hotel, exhausted, and immediately fell asleep.

I'm sure they will come back and then I'll tell them everything I know. I won't try to lie or to protect myself. What good would it do? After all, those memories, that drifting . . . none of it belongs to me anymore.

*

"You don't look well, Antoine."

"No."

"Are you sick?"

"No . . . I mean, yes, maybe . . . I don't know."

"Things aren't going well with Judith?"

"Yes . . . I . . . I don't know."

Antoine is sitting with Séverine in a café near the Odéon. He'd explained to Judith that he needed to be alone, that he was going to walk for a while.

Séverine's face seems gentle to him, nearly childlike compared with Judith's tormented intensity. He'd like to confide in her. But how to explain? Where to begin? She would have had to know already, would have to have known from the outset. She looks at him, her sad eyes still trying to smile. All she wants is to help him. She doesn't say so, but he knows. And that, more than anything else, frightens him. Maybe because he feels he has no right to Séverine's kindness, because her concern reminds him that he's an impostor. Maybe too because he realizes that neither she nor anyone else can do anything for him now.

To be forsaken by her would be unbearable. He would like her to hold onto only the oldest memories. He would like to say to her: What you will read in the papers isn't me. I've never been that person; I've only been the person whom you knew. Antoine would have liked her to forget everything about him. He would have liked it if only a very small image, ordinary and inconsequential, stayed inside her, the memory for instance of their breakfasts in a little crêperie near the port of Cannes, where the owner, a stout and jovial woman, would greet them with, "How are the lovebirds this morning?" They didn't say much during those breakfasts, but the silence was light and they did not feel a need to fill it. Antoine thinks to himself now that this silence may be precisely what they shared. Séverine would from now on be its guardian.

Across the street, Judith watches them. She followed Antoine, saw him go into the café, go to the table where Séverine was sitting, then join her on the bench. Leaning against the wall, she doesn't think about the cold that is getting into her limbs, or about the fine rain that is drizzling down her face. She doesn't try to imagine what they are saying, doesn't wonder how often they've seen each other since Antoine and she have been together, doesn't even try to tell herself that she should have suspected it. She feels nothing, neither hate nor anger nor disappointment. Motionless, she looks at them.

Half an hour later Antoine gets up. He knows that if he stays any longer his resolve will be shaken. Just as he is giving Séverine a peck on the cheek he remembers the last day of vacation in Cannes some twelve years earlier. They had gone walking in a small park at the end of rue d'Antibes. The next day, he was supposed to go back to Paris and as he was leaving her, he'd been on the point of kissing her on the mouth. At the last moment he'd changed his mind, either out of cowardice or in order not to break the peaceful spell that had brought them together that summer. This time, again, a thought crosses his mind. It's not really a desire, a question rather: "What would she say, what would I feel if I kissed her?" And this time again, at the last minute, he decides not to. But from the gentleness of her eyes that follow every move he makes, from the firmness of her hands on his shoulders, and above all the warmth of her cheek pressed against his face, Antoine realizes that Séverine might not have pushed him away.

*

Pont du Garigliano, Paris, 16 November 2002

Three a.m. A young man in his mid-twenties is walking towards the Pont du Garigliano. His shirt collar is open, the rain is streaming down his face, his jacket, too large for him, is soaking wet. He can't wait to get home. An hour ago he still felt lighthearted, but the happy, all-powerful thoughts brought on by wine have gradually faded away and the future that seemed so malleable a few moments earlier is now closing inexorably on him. His head aches. Silence is buzzing in his ears.

He just has to cross the bridge and at the corner of the next street he'll be home. He walks faster and faster. The cold wind makes him shiver. He thinks to himself, "I'm chilled to the bones. I'm stupid, really, I should have worn my overcoat."

Some fifty paces away, in the yellow light of the streetlamps, he sees a man, motionless, who seems to be leaning against the parapet. "Drunk," he thinks. "I'd better cross the street." He slows down, then stops short. The man is actually standing on the other side of the parapet. Hands behind his back, head bent forward, his body is rocking slightly as if pushed by the wind or absorbed in prayer. Coming closer, the young man notices another shape, the outline of a woman standing beside him. They seem to be holding hands.

The young man is afraid. He would like to retrace his steps, start to run, but he doesn't want to attract their attention. He stands there, still, frightened by what is about to happen and terrified by his own helplessness. The young woman's long black hair, tangled and blown by the wind, hides her face. She seems to be leaning towards the man, she murmurs something in his ear. "That's it," thinks the young man, "they're going to jump."

But they stand there, as if paralyzed. The young man imagines them gazing at the water, at the few glimmers of light carried on the river's dark waves. Suddenly he hears the piercing howl of a siren a few streets away. He notices a bluish light travelling along the

Seine. When he turns around the man is no longer there. He has heard nothing, not the slightest cry. He looks at the woman, standing still, her chest slightly thrown out—what is she waiting for to join him? Unable to make out her features he imagines her hesitating, then filling her lungs one last time, eyes closed, frozen in a tragic expression. The young man no longer feels the wind lashing his face, he has forgotten that he's tired, is no longer dreaming about his warm and cozy bed. He is thinking about just one thing: to get close to the woman, take her hand and comfort her without asking any questions. He sees himself already sitting with her in a café, a cup of hot tea in her hand. She cries, she smiles at him, she is grateful. He doesn't know her, but already her long black hair, her shining eyes, bright and mischievous, seem familiar to him. Soon, he's sure of it, she will talk to him about confidence and treachery, about hopes nearly grasped, happiness scarcely lived, constantly postponed. She will talk to him about the man she lost and then got back, about everything they had desired and everything that was impossible. Suddenly the young man is pulled from his daydream: the woman has turned around, she has straddled the parapet again and like a sleepwalker obeying the secret voices of her dream, she is walking towards him, her head down, hands stuffed in the pockets of her raincoat. The young man is on the verge of approaching her; surely she will look up at him, she will stop, wait for him to make the first move. But she doesn't slow down as she comes closer to him. She meets him without even a glance and continues on her way, looking determined, absorbed in thought. Speechless he watches her walk away. He would like to call her, follow her, catch up with her: maybe he can help her, walk her home? But she's already too far away. Tomorrow he will remember nothing—at most, the image of a young woman with black hair standing on a bridge will continue to wander in his mind for a few moments. And maybe a question too: was she really crying or was it just the rain streaming down her cheeks?